'I can't *do* thi[...]

Charli actually st[...]
women do this al[...]

Her distress finally spurred Grant into
motion. 'Let's see.'

As he patiently fastened the tiny hooks,
Charli watched her breasts gradually fill the
bustier's cups and swell over their scalloped
tops like rising bread dough. She crossed her
arms over her chest.

'I've seen you, remember?' he murmured,
gently pulling her arms away.

His hands seemed to generate some kind
of electric current as they glided up to her
shoulders. His head dipped and he nuzzled
her hair. In the mirror, she watched her lips
part, her nostrils flare.

His words were a scalding whisper against her
scalp. 'How could I have ever thought…'
With a ragged sigh, he pressed a kiss to her
hair. 'You're more woman than I ever could
have imagined. God, I must've been blind.
Or crazy. Or both.'

Dear Reader,

When four romantically minded school girls vow to find each other husbands if any of them are still single at age thirty, they have no idea how complicated it will make their lives twelve years later!

In *I Do, But Here's the Catch*, Grant wants only to make partner in his stuffy law firm—and that won't happen unless he finds himself a wife. Thus he enters into a marriage of convenience with unassuming schoolteacher Charli, a marriage that becomes decidedly inconvenient when he can't seem to remember that he's not attracted to her!

THE WEDDING RING matchmaking pact was set into motion last month in *Love's Funny That Way*, when Raven Muldoon fell in love with the brother of the man her pals had chosen as her future husband. Next month you can read Sunny's story in *One Eager Bride To Go*, when a devastating secret will threaten the happiness of reunited school sweethearts. Finally, in January, two-time divorcée Amanda, determined to remain single, will try to outwit her matchmaking friends with a phony fiancé in *Fiancé For Hire*.

I hope you'll join me for all of these fun, sexy WEDDING RING stories. You can visit me on the Web at www.pamelaburford.com, or write to me (include an SAE with return postage) at PO Box 1321, North Baldwin, NY 11510-1721, USA.

Love,

Pamela Burford

I DO, BUT HERE'S THE CATCH

by

Pamela Burford

MILLS & BOON®

To my wonderful mother-in-law, Lore Loeser.

*First published in Great Britain 2001
by Harlequin Mills & Boon Limited,
Eton House, 18-24 Paradise Road, Richmond, Surrey TW9 1SR*

© Pamela Burford Loeser 2001

ISBN 0 263 82824 7

21-1101

*Printed and bound in Spain
by Litografía Rosés S.A., Barcelona*

1

"You never met this man?"

"Mama, I told you, it's a blind date." Charli Rossi pawed through her jewelry box, a relic from her childhood, like almost everything else in the tiny bedroom under the eaves that she'd once shared with her two sisters.

She still remembered how proud and grown-up she'd felt at age ten when Grandma and Grandpa Rossi had given her the fancy box for Christmas. Now, twenty years later, the glossy ivory and gold paint had long since yellowed and chipped; the floral decals had mostly worn away.

"I can't wear any of this junk!" Charli emptied the jewelry box onto her narrow twin bed. "Mama, can I borrow your pearl studs? Please!"

"What's wrong with what you have?" Mama lifted a pair of blue enameled button earrings from the pink chenille bedspread and held them up to Charli's ears.

"Oh, Mama, I can't wear those!"

"Why not? Robby gave you these for your sweet sixteen," she said, referring to one of Charli's five brothers. "They suit you."

Charli glanced at her image in the dressing-table mirror, which had been in need of resilvering for as long as she could remember. Yes, she thought glumly, the dowdy earrings did indeed suit her. As did the dress she'd chosen, a matronly cornflower-blue shirt-waist printed with tiny white blossoms. The hem fell to an awkward level a couple of inches below her knees, too long to be youthful, too short to be, well, youthful. The low-heeled beige pumps didn't help.

Raven Muldoon, one of her three closest friends, always wore calf-length or longer skirts, and they always looked wonderful on her, casual yet somehow sophisticated. Amanda Coppersmith often wore short skirts with her elegant suits, exposing her knees and shapely legs. And Sunny Bleecker...well, Sunny had an eclectic style all her own, when she wasn't wearing her hideous, bright-pink waitress uniform.

Facing her drab reflection, Charli had to admit that the most flattering outfit she owned was the black tuxedo-like pantsuit she wore during high school concerts, while conducting the ninety-eight students in the school's elite symphonic band.

Her hair was dark brown and hung stick-straight just past her shoulder blades. This evening she'd parted it in the middle and pulled back the sides with simple tortoiseshell barrettes.

As for her face, she now wished she'd left well enough—or homely enough—alone. She'd experimented with a little blusher and a dab of rose-colored lipstick, and she wasn't used to seeing that much color on her olive complexion. Nor could she get used to the sight of her lashes glopped up with mascara. Just one more thing to feel awkward about tonight, to worry about.

She checked her watch. Too late to change clothes,

even if she owned something more stylish, which she didn't. Too late to scrub off the makeup. "And your pearl choker, too," she told Mama, not waiting for permission, but racing out of her room to her parents' across the hall.

Mama was right behind her. "Take my pink cardigan. I'd lend you my good white one, but you can't wear white till after Memorial Day. And Easter isn't even for two more weeks."

Charli groaned inwardly. "I'm wearing the beige linen jacket Amanda helped me pick out."

"The blazer? That's too businesslike. He'll think you're a cold fish."

And if I wear your cardigan, Charli thought, *he'll think I'm his mother*. Or someone's maiden aunt, which was precisely what she was. To be depressingly accurate, she was now a maiden *great-aunt*, courtesy of her married nephew, John, who'd become the father of twins last year. Charli fumbled with the clasp on the choker.

"You've got yourself all worked up," Mama declared. "Let this strange man you don't even know worry about impressing *you!*"

Charli inserted the pearl post earrings as she sprinted downstairs to await the doorbell. The last thing she wanted was her blind date having to wait for her on the plastic-wrapped living room sofa, enduring Papa's interrogation. Halfway down the stairs she abruptly reversed direction—she'd forgotten her jacket.

"Well, knock me over, why don't you?" Mama complained.

"You don't have to *follow* me!" Charli snapped, veering around her to pound back up the steps.

"Don't talk to your mother like that!" Papa hollered from the kitchen. "Betty, leave the girl alone. She hasn't had a date in three years and four months!"

Well, thank you so much for keeping the neighbors up-to-date. Where was the jacket? It was supposed to be on the back of her dressing-table chair—she knew she'd left it on the back of her dressing-table chair! She did a three-sixty in her room, rifled through her closet.

"Where's my jacket! Mama, did you move my jacket?"

"I didn't do anything with your jacket!" Mama screeched from downstairs. "Wear my cardigan. And take my pink straw handbag—it's on the shelf in my closet. There's the doorbell. I'll let him in."

Oh, God! Charli had counted on meeting him at the door and slipping out quickly.

Sounds of conversation drifted from downstairs. Charli heard Mama's high, grating voice, even louder than usual as she ushered her daughter's date into the house.

Where's that jacket! Charli dashed into the cramped, faux-wood-paneled bathroom and checked the robe hooks, from which dangled Papa's faded green terry robe, Mama's striped housedress and Grandma's support hose. No jacket. Perspiration gathered under her arms as she ran back to her room for another search. Could she get away without it? No. It was mid-April, and still pretty nippy at night.

As she tore her room apart, she heard Papa's coarse Brooklynese, along with a deeper, well-modulated, refined-sounding voice she'd never heard before. Papa must have said something Mama didn't like, because she started squawking at him like an angry hen. Grandma's Italian-accented voice joined the mix, snarling at her son and daughter-in-law to mind their manners in front of Carlotta's fella.

Carlotta's fella! Oh, God, please tell me she didn't say that!

Charli sank heavily onto her creaky little bed. She dropped her head into her hands. Why even try? She should have known back in high school, when she and her three best friends had shared the sacred handclasp that established the Wedding Ring matchmaking pact, that their efforts were doomed to failure, at least as far as she was concerned.

True, it had worked for Raven, even when she'd muddied the waters by falling in love with the *brother* of the man the other three had chosen for her. It had ended happily, though—Raven and Hunter had returned from their honeymoon that very day. The Wedding Ring's first success. But Charli wasn't Raven; she didn't have Raven's self-confidence, or outgoing personality, or looks. Charli didn't have anything to hold a man's interest.

Downstairs, the sounds of squabbling had ceased. Charli's nape prickled. If her parents weren't fighting, that most likely meant someone was engaged in conversation with "Carlotta's fella."

With a defeated sigh, she rose and shambled into her parents' room, where she extracted Mama's pink cardigan from the high chest of drawers. She descended the stairs, wishing this accursed date were already behind her.

"What line of work are you in?" she heard Papa ask.

The smooth, cultured voice answered, "I'm an attorney. I've been with Farman, Van Cleave and Holm for five years now."

"No kiddin'. You down there on Wall Street?"

"Yes."

"No kiddin'."

At the bottom of the stairs, Charli took a deep breath. She composed her features and crossed the small entrance foyer to the living room, reserved strictly for company. It had always been reserved strictly for company, even during Charli's childhood, when this small house on Long Island's South Shore had been crammed to the rafters with ten people.

Papa was doing his lord-of-the-manor imitation, holding forth from a chintz-covered wing chair. Grandma Rossi—the rotund, black-clad doyenne of the family—was perched on the other wing chair, her sensible shoes not quite touching the carpet, her iron-gray hair scraped back into its usual bun. Charli's gaze homed in on the gentleman sitting on one end of the shrink-wrapped sofa.

What struck her immediately was his maturity; he appeared to be around forty. The last time she'd gone out with a man—yes, over three years earlier—both she and her date had been twenty-six. That had been Tim McMurty, a divorced plumbing contractor and the son of one of Papa's fishing buddies. Tim hadn't called her again. She'd heard he'd remarried.

Charli stepped into the living room. Her date noticed her. After the first, fleeting instant, he concealed his disappointment like a gentleman, rising with a flat, polite smile, his hand extended. Charli wanted to slink back upstairs, pull her quilt over her head and hibernate for a month.

"You must be Charli," he said. "I'm Grant Sterling." He was around six feet tall, with neatly trimmed, light brown hair and a direct hazel gaze that she suspected didn't miss much. He wore a heathery-gray silk blazer over a white linen shirt and gray slacks. No necktie—the shirt was open at the throat.

She forced herself to return his smile. "It's nice to meet you."

Mama bustled in, carrying a tray laden with a Pepperidge Farm cookie assortment and her best china dessert plates. "Coffee will be ready in a minute."

"Mama, we can't stay for coffee," Charli said, scooting into the entrance hall and snatching her brown shoulder bag off the console table.

"I told you to take my pink straw handbag! That brown thing looks like luggage!" Mama set the tray on the coffee table. "You have time for a cookie. Sit. We'll talk, get to know one another."

"We have reservations," Charli blurted, and looked quickly at Grant, wondering if it was true. She had no idea where he was taking her.

He turned to Mama. "That's right, Mrs. Rossi. If we're even five minutes late for our eight-o'clock dinner reservations, we lose them. And with that construction they're doing on the Cross Island Parkway, it could take us a while to get into the city."

"You're going to the city?" asked Papa, who hadn't

been to Manhattan since John Glenn's ticker-tape parade in '62. "There's plenty of nice restaurants out here on the Island."

"You have time for one cookie," Mama insisted. "Sit."

Grandma spoke up. "Betty, they don't have time. *Lasciarli andare!* Let them go!"

"One cookie!"

Grant made a show of checking his watch. With a rueful shrug he said, "I'm afraid I'll have to take a rain check. Thanks anyway, Mrs. Rossi." He thrust out his hand to Papa, who heaved his bulk out of the wing chair. "It was a pleasure, sir."

"Likewise." Papa shook Grant's hand, clearly impressed by his manners. "When are you gonna have her home?"

Grandma tossed her arms skyward. "Carlotta's a grown woman, Joey. She'll be home when she's home."

He stabbed his chest with a blunt finger. "I'm her father!"

"She's thirty years old!" Mama screeched, while Grandma winced at her daughter-in-law's indiscretion. "She doesn't have to be home by eleven."

Charli thought Grant would be happy to have her home by nine, but all she said as she backed toward the front door was, "Don't wait up."

Outside, it was nearly dark, and cool enough that Charli was forced to put on Mama's stodgy pink cardigan. Grant opened the passenger door of the silver Infiniti sedan parked at the curb, and she slid onto the chilly, leather-upholstered seat. Neither of them said anything as he got in behind the wheel and pulled out, headed for the highway. Charli fought the impulse to apologize. This couldn't have been what Grant had anticipated when he'd agreed to this blind date.

What had Raven told him about her? And what on earth had made Raven think that a worldly, sophisticated man like Grant Sterling would be interested in someone like Charli?

Finally she broke the silence. "Thanks for helping me get us out of there. My parents can be a little...overinvolved."

"No problem. One of the hazards of living with your folks, I suppose."

Something in his tone needled her. "They need someone to take care of them," she said. "Mama and Papa are both in their seventies. And Nonni, my grandma, she's ninety-three."

Grant glanced at her as he pulled onto the highway entrance ramp. "So they were in their forties when they had you?"

She nodded. "I'm the youngest of eight children."

"Don't any of your siblings help out?"

"Not really. They all live nearby, but they're all married, with families of their own. They're too busy, so—" she shrugged "—it's up to me. I don't mind." Charli didn't tell him the rest, that in her family's strict view, "nice" unmarried daughters didn't leave home to set up their own households. It simply wasn't done. She felt compelled to add, "It's not as if taking care of them is my whole life."

"Raven said you're a teacher?"

"I teach instrumental music at Courtland Park High School. My alma mater."

Grant emitted a grunt of interest, feigned, no doubt. She sensed he was casting about for a politely enthusiastic comment, and that irked her. Her work gave her enormous satisfaction; it was the one arena in which she consistently felt confident, productive and appreciated. She might not be some hotshot Wall Street lawyer like Grant Sterling, but that didn't mean her career didn't deserve respect.

But she couldn't think of a way to convey her pride that didn't sound defensive and unladylike, and the moment passed. It was just as well. What he must already think of her!

They didn't talk much during the remainder of the ride into Manhattan. Grant didn't even try to find a space on the street, but pulled into a pricey parking garage a half block from the restaurant he'd chosen. Charli's eyes grew round when she saw where he'd brought her.

"You don't like Japanese?" he asked.

"I don't know. I've never had it."

He showed no surprise.

"Well, I had a chicken teriyaki salad once. In a little bistro near the school." Charli had never set foot in a Japanese restaurant.

"It's strictly sushi here," Grant said. "No grilled dishes. Bad choice?"

He must have thought she was the most unsophisticated woman he'd ever met. Everyone ate sushi nowadays. It had been standard fare in New York for the past couple of decades. Raven and Amanda dined at the local sushi restaurant all the time. Amanda had actually taken a class to learn how to make it. Even Sunny, whose tastes ran to burgers and fries, had tried it a few times.

With a patience bordering on condescension, he said, "We can go somewhere else."

Charli's throat felt tight; heat stung her cheeks. "No. You made reservations. And—and I've been meaning to try sushi."

Grant's patience began to slip. "It's no problem. We'll go somewhere else." He hauled a tiny cellular phone out of his breast pocket and thumbed a button; it beeped. "Do you like steak?"

"I said I'd like to eat here, Grant." Charli pulled open the door of the restaurant and looked at him expectantly. After a moment he slipped the phone back in his pocket and held the door for her.

The interior of the restaurant was elegant and exotic, marked by soft lighting and clean lines. Lilting Asian music played softly in the background. Blond wood predominated, along with Japanese prints and silk hangings. The aromas were subtle, alien, not unpleasant. A kimono-clad hostess showed them to their table, which was set low to the floor in a booth separated from others by paper shoji screens.

Grant slipped off his loafers and placed them at the edge of the booth, leaving his feet clad in thin, charcoal-gray socks.

Charli looked at the low table in dismay. "We're supposed to sit on the floor?"

"When in Tokyo..."

There were regular tables, too, the kind with chairs.

Grant could have asked for one of them, for her sake, but he didn't, and she couldn't bring herself to speak up.

He waited while she removed her pumps. Charli wished the left heel of her panty hose didn't have a small hole sealed by a dollop of clear nail polish. She experienced a funny jolt seeing her shoes set neatly next to Grant's. The little tableau looked deceptively intimate.

Grant offered his hand as she lowered herself onto the straw tatami mat that covered the floor. First she tried keeping her legs together, tucking them to one side, but that was awkward and uncomfortable. Clumsily she shifted into a cross-legged position, pulling her skirt around her knees.

With a fluid grace, he settled opposite her as a waitress arrived to present menus and take their drink order. She set down a small bamboo dish containing two rolled white washcloths.

"Have you ever tried sake?" Grant asked Charli.

"No, but I've always wanted to." This was, in fact, true, although she doubted he believed her.

Grant ordered the sake, and the waitress left them.

Charli smiled lamely, racking her brain for something to say. "So you're one of Raven's hypnotherapy clients? Oh." She covered her mouth, wishing she'd kept it shut.

Her chagrin seemed to amuse him. "Am I supposed to be embarrassed about trying hypnosis to help improve my golf swing?" He handed her a startlingly hot washcloth and unrolled the other for his own use.

"Well, I guess not." She followed his lead, wiping

her hands with the cloth and depositing it back on the little dish. "I just thought, you know, it's a kind of therapy. Maybe you didn't want anyone to know."

"God help me if that's my most intriguing secret. Let's see." He opened the menu. "The young lady has never eaten raw fish."

Did he have to put it like that? She'd been trying not to think of it as raw fish.

Call it sushi. Everyone eats sushi.

Against her will, her eyes strayed to the little display card on the table, showing photographs of the restaurant's various offerings, one of which was clearly octopus. A raw little tentacle with suckers and everything. She wondered if it clung to the plate when you tried to eat it.

"I offered you steak," he said.

Charli jerked her gaze from the card. She hated the look on his face, outwardly benign but with a touch of smugness that rankled the heck out of her.

On impulse she asked, "Were you raised in Japan?"

His eyebrows drew together. "No."

"Then chances are you remember your first taste of raw fish."

He studied her a moment. "Point taken. There's a first time for everything. Ah, here's our sake."

As Grant poured the liquid from a small ceramic flask into a tiny matching cup, he explained that while most people think of sake as a wine, it's actually a kind of beer, being fermented from rice, a grain.

Charli lifted the cup and took an experimental sip, mildly surprised to find the drink warm and smooth,

sliding easily down her throat with the barest alco-
holic bite. She smiled. "I like it."

The corners of Grant's eyes crinkled as he topped
off her cup. "A little Dutch courage for the ordeal to
come."

He really was quite attractive, Charli thought, when
he smiled like that. It softened the stern lines of his
face and hinted at something almost gentle within
him. His eyes were that changeable hazel hue that
never looked the same twice. They were dark now, in
the muted lighting, almost the same pewter shade as
his sport coat.

Charli found her gaze drawn to the modest amount
of skin exposed by the open collar of his shirt. There
was something uncompromisingly masculine about
the sinewy neck and Adam's apple, the hollow of his
throat and the light dusting of hair just visible in the V
of white linen. She was careful not to stare too openly.

Grant seemed content to sit quietly, sipping his
sake. He didn't fill the air with ceaseless chatter, and
for that Charli was grateful. He regarded her with polite interest, and she couldn't help but wonder what he
saw. A frumpy, old-maid schoolteacher who lived
with her parents? Or was it possible there was something about her that he found appealing? Her features
were ordinary but not offensive, with the exception of
her nose, just big enough to dominate the rest of her
face. She knew it had to be the first thing people noticed.

Her body was nothing to crow about, either. She'd
often wished she had Amanda's figure, tall and
model-slim. Though her measurements were more or

less average, Charli was on the short side, five-three, which probably explained why she looked dumpy no matter what she wore.

She turned her attention to the menu, with its mysterious references to sashimi and *maki* and— What on earth was a hand roll? "Any suggestions?" she asked.

"I'll order for us both." Grant signaled the waitress. "I'll get an assortment—you can try everything."

Great. Visions of octopus tentacles flashed through her mind.

When the lacquered platter of sushi arrived, blessedly devoid of tentacles, Charli had to admit it looked awfully pretty: pastel-hued strips of fish arranged on little beds of sticky rice, alongside piles of shaved ginger and green wasabi mustard. There were also round slices of *maki,* fish rolled up with rice and dark seaweed, some studded with sesame seeds, others with red caviar. She recognized cucumber and avocado in some of the *maki,* and was surprised to discover that a portion of it featured, not raw fish at all, but cooked shrimp and crab.

Grant refused to let her restrict herself to the cooked variety, however. With his chopsticks he lifted a piece of sushi, dipped it in the tiny bowl of soy sauce and held it near her mouth.

She stared at the slender tidbit of dark pink fish on its nest of white rice. "Um, what is it?"

"Tuna. It's very mild. Try it."

He wielded the chopsticks so proficiently. Charli had never gotten the hang of them herself; nevertheless, she started to take them from him. He shooed her hand away and moved the food closer to her lips. She looked at him. He was watching her closely, a curious glint in his eye.

Charli met his stare. If this high-handed man expected to be entertained by the sight of his sheltered bumpkin of a date struggling to choke down uncooked flesh, she refused to put on a show for him.

Charli's senses went on red alert as she leaned slightly forward and closed her mouth over the piece of sushi. If the sight of their shoes side by side had been disturbingly intimate, the act of eating directly from his chopsticks was practically sexual. Mustering her courage, she bit the sushi in half and began chewing.

To her surprise, the fish was indeed mildly flavored, almost overpowered by the salty soy sauce. More surprisingly, it was exceedingly tender. For some reason, she'd expected a chewy blob that would fight her all the way. After a few moments she relaxed and gave herself over to the experience.

Grant's perceptive gaze never left her face. He watched her chew, and swallow, and look expectantly at the piece of sushi still clamped between his chopsticks. There was that gentle smile again as he offered it to her.

After she'd downed that bit, too, he said, "I take it the verdict is positive?"

"So far." Sipping her sake, she peered intently at the pretty arrangement. "What should I try next?"

"Well, since you've discovered a fondness for tuna, why don't you have a go at the *tekka maki?*" He pointed out one of the rolled-up pieces.

Charli fumbled with her chopsticks, finally lifting it,

only to have it slip from her grasp and plop into the bowl of soy sauce. Finally she managed to bring it to her mouth. She started to bite into it, and Grant said, "No, eat the whole thing at once."

It was more than her usual mouthful, but she complied, shoving the entire thing in and feeling her face heat as she envisioned how bovine she must look chewing that big wad of food. It was, however, absolutely delicious—surprisingly delicious.

Who knew?

Only millions of people around the world, Charli had to admit, while she'd taken the safe route all these years and avoided even trying the Japanese delicacy.

Taking the safe route was something she had a lot of experience with, but lately she'd been forced to question whether it had served her well. It had been Grandma Rossi, Charli's lifelong confidante, who had finally spurred her to action on the romantic front, encouraging her to cooperate with the Wedding Ring and let her closest friends introduce her to a potential future husband.

Always you think about duty, never about yourself, Nonni had told Charli during Raven and Hunter's wedding. You're a good girl, Carlotta, but sometimes you gotta think about yourself. Even when it's a lot less scary to think about duty.

Charli washed down the *tekka maki* with another sip of sake. The drink was deliciously warming and she drained the cup. No longer needing Mama's sweater, she slipped out of it, wriggling a little to get the sleeves off. The movement drew Grant's gaze to her chest for a fleeting instant.

Smoothly he refilled her cup and asked, "So you come home from the school every day and do housework?"

"Well, yeah, but it's a lot more than housework. For one thing, someone always has to go to the doctor—or the dentist, optometrist, podiatrist, you name it. Mama has to see a physical therapist twice a week for her sciatica. Papa goes to the chiropractor for a compressed disk. And Nonni's always at the cardiologist or the rheumatologist or the orthopedist."

"And it's up to you to take them everywhere?" He popped a piece of yellowish sushi into his mouth and motioned for her to do the same.

"Sure." She grappled with the chopsticks. "Between their declining vision and their various medical problems, neither of my parents drives anymore. You wouldn't believe how challenging it can be, juggling all the appointments. I have a system, though—it involves sticky notes and different colored pens and a master calendar I refer to as my Bible. Somehow it all works out."

"So you're the designated chauffeur."

"When I'm not handling the household finances," she said, "the bills and taxes and insurance and bank accounts, all of that. All the shopping, too, of course—groceries, clothes, medications. I keep up the property and make sure everything gets repaired and painted and whatnot."

"You must possess exceptional organizational skills."

He sounded genuinely impressed, prompting her to chuckle. "You don't know the half of it. Have you ever made Thanksgiving dinner for thirty hungry relatives? Or a ninetieth birthday party for eighty guests? I had to rent the Knights of Columbus hall for that one, but I did all the cooking myself."

His eyes widened. "You cooked for eighty people?"

"Five courses plus the cake. It was exhausting, but it was worth it. And I do love to cook. And entertain. So for me it's not work."

"Still—all that on top of your full-time job." He shook his head, incredulous.

She shrugged. "It's got to be done. My folks gave me life, took care of me when I was tiny and helpless. The least I can do is make sure they're comfortable and cared for now, when they need me."

Gradually they worked their way through the large sushi platter, as well as the sake. Charli was feeling pleasantly relaxed, even a little tipsy. She asked Grant what kind of law he practiced.

"Matrimonial mostly."

"Oh. You mean like divorces? That's so sad."

"Not at the rates my firm bills."

That remark was obviously meant to be witty, so Charli dutifully smiled, while privately she couldn't help but wonder if it ever bothered him, earning a living from people's shattered dreams.

She said, "I overheard you telling my father you've been with your firm for five years. What did you do before that?"

"I was an ADA—an assistant in the Manhattan district attorney's office." He smiled. "Prosecuting bad guys."

"How did you get from there to divorce work?"

"After I graduated law school, I clerked for two years with a judge handling matrimonial cases, so I got experience in that area. And the partner who recruited me at Farman, Van Cleave was impressed by my litigation background—he felt I was well suited to handling their high-profile divorce cases."

She noticed him furtively checking his watch. As little experience as Charli had with dating, she was more than familiar with that particular signal. She set down her sake cup. "Do you have to be somewhere? Because it's okay if you do," she added quickly.

He looked at her, and the truth kicked her in the gut. She hadn't misread the gesture. Or his intention to cut the evening short. She saw it in his eyes.

"Because I really should get home," she said, twisting the napkin in her lap. "I really didn't want to be out too late tonight."

He stared at her for long moments, his gaze too insightful for comfort. His eyes were greenish-gray now. She looked away.

A busboy removed their dishes. From the booth behind Charli came a burst of masculine laughter. Across the aisle, a Japanese couple ordered dinner in their native language. Charli waited for Grant to signal the waitress for the check.

At last he said, softly, "Your grandma says you can stay out as late as you like."

Charli glanced at him. His expression was neutral; only his eyes held the trace of a teasing smile. Was he making fun of her? While she groped for a response, he said, "Have you ever been to Bunny's?"

"What's Bunny's?"

"A club in the west Twenties. One of my clients is performing there tonight."

"Oh. No, I've never been there." Or to any club, but no doubt he surmised that.

"It's a private show, to promote his new album," he said. "By invitation only. We can get dessert there." Now he did signal the waitress.

Charli might not have a lot going for her in the romance department, but she had her pride. They both knew where he wanted to take her, and it wasn't to any club—it was right to her doorstep.

"I'd prefer to go home, Grant." She made herself look him in the eye. "I hope that doesn't disrupt your plans."

Grant started to say something, and stopped. She detected a morsel of contrition, which only made it worse. She didn't want him to feel guilty for unloading his dreary blind date this early in the evening, and she sure as heck didn't want him feeling sorry for her!

The check arrived. Without so much as glancing at it, he thrust a platinum credit card at the waitress, who spirited it away. "Did I mention it's Phil Rivera?"

"Who? You mean...?" Phil Rivera was a well-known singer who'd gone solo when his band broke up last year. "That's your client? The one who's performing at Bunny's?"

Grant nodded. "I worked on his divorce. He's very grateful. Considering his probable future earnings, the settlement could've been disastrous. It wasn't."

Charli recalled having heard something about Rivera ending a sixteen-year marriage to the mother of his three children. So Grant had been his attorney.

Charli knew that divorce proceedings were generally skewed in favor of the wealthier party, in most cases the husband. Apparently Grant derived great satisfaction from chiseling down alimony and child-support payments on behalf of his wealthy clients.

He asked, "Do you like Rivera's music?"

"I do, yes. But I have to decline. I can take the train home. You can still make the show."

He gaped at her. "The *train?*"

"It's less than an hour's ride."

"You think I'd let you take the train home?"

"Look, it's no big deal—"

"That's not how it works, Charli. I picked you up, I'll drop you off." The waitress appeared with the charge slip. Grant scrawled the total and his signature, barely taking his eyes off Charli. "Half an hour," he said. "Give it half an hour at the club. Then, if you still want to go home, I'll take you right home."

"It's not— I don't—" Why did he have to make this so difficult?

"One song. We'll stay for one song." Rising, he came around the table and offered his hand. "Don't forget your sweater."

2

"SETH, THIS IS the nonsmoking section," Charli called over to the trumpet section leader.

The high school AIDS benefit concert had just ended, and about half of the ninety-eight members of the symphonic band had descended on Wafflemania, the local greasy-spoon diner. All the students wore the requisite black tuxedo pants, pleated white shirt, blue satin cummerbund and matching bow tie—except for the girls, whose collars sported blue satin rosettes. Charli shared a table with Raven and Amanda, who had attended the concert and decided to join the band at their favorite hangout afterward.

Raven sipped her chocolate egg cream, one eye on Seth, who was puffing away. "He's pretending he didn't hear you."

Charli sighed. "Guess I've gotta go over there and play the heavy."

Amanda, stirring her jasmine tea, said, "Something tells me you needn't bother."

Charli watched as their friend Sunny, in her short-skirted, hot-pink waitress uniform, calmly deposited a round of sodas on Seth's table, snatched the cigarette out of his mouth and dropped it in his water glass.

"Hey!" he barked as his buddies guffawed.

"How do you have enough wind for your horn," she asked, "with your lungs full of tar?"

"Oh, I've got enough wind for a lot of things," the seventeen-year-old blustered. He wagged his eyebrows salaciously. "Use your imagination."

"Careful, Seth," Brad Davidson warned, with a nervous glance at Charli. "She's Ms. Rossi's friend."

In a lightning move, Sunny grabbed Seth's little finger and held on tight, bending it back just enough to secure his undivided attention. "I'm using my imagination," she said pleasantly. "I imagine you need this finger for that fancy valve work."

Seth's friends hooted their glee. Red-faced, he demanded, "Let go of me, you b—"

"Uh-uh-uh, is that any way to talk to the lady who's been making sure your fries are extra-crispy since you were in kindergarten?" She bent the pinky back just a tad more. "This is the clean-air section, Seth. I don't want to breathe your smoke, even if it's filtered through your lungs first. Did you want toast or a muffin with that omelette?" she asked Brad.

Charli chewed back a grin as she watched her friend put the audacious pup in his place. That was Sunny, supremely comfortable dealing with all sorts of people. Perhaps it came with the territory—she'd been waitressing at Wafflemania since the day after their high school graduation. But somehow Charli knew that even if it had been her wearing that hideous uniform for twelve years, she'd never have Sunny's self-confidence or her way with people.

"That outfit looks sharp on you," Amanda told Charli. "Dramatic. Sexy."

Charli looked down at the tuxedo pantsuit. "You tell me that at every concert."

"You should wear black more often," Amanda said. "Pants, too. We'll go shopping—I'll help you pick out some new things."

"That's just what they need to see me in at the school," Charli said, with a wry smile. "Something dramatic and sexy."

Amanda was forever offering to help Charli shop for clothes, and Charli was forever declining. Amanda's preference for black no doubt stemmed from the fact that the color looked sensational on her, with her pale blond hair and willowy figure. If Charli put on a black dress, she'd look like Grandma Rossi.

Raven said gently, "There's more to life than the school, Charli. Maybe you should let her take you shopping."

"What did you wear for your date last night?" Amanda asked.

"Oh, just one of the dresses I wear to work." Charli bit back a smile, remembering last night.

Eagle-eyed Amanda shot forward in her seat. "Details, girl. I want details."

Grinning now, Charli dropped her burning face into her hands.

"Oh, now I *really* want details!" Amanda crowed.

"Shh!" Charli glanced around the room, filled with her music students.

"Down, girl," Raven told Amanda, but she, too, was grinning.

Charli knew her giddy excitement was plain for all

to see. "There isn't that much to tell," she said, only to have her pals chorus a suggestive "Uh-huhhh..."

Sunny materialized by the table, coffee carafe in hand. "First things first. Where did he take you?"

"To a Japanese restaurant to start. I tried sushi."

Amanda blinked. "You?"

"And sake."

"Candy is dandy," Sunny purred, "but liquor is quicker."

"Oh, stop," Charli said, feeling her face grow hotter.

"Lucky you," Amanda said. "Grant Sterling, Esquire, is quite the hunk." Raven had introduced Grant to Sunny and Amanda first, so they could approve the choice.

The four of them had formed the Wedding Ring twelve years earlier, during their senior year of high school. The Ring existed for one purpose only. If any member was unmarried at age thirty, the other three—her best friends in the world—would find her a husband. The rules were simple: while they were dating, the man in question must not be told he was part of a formal matchmaking scheme; and as long as he remained interested, the Ring member had to continue seeing him for at least three months.

The approach of their thirtieth birthdays this year had found all four friends unmarried. Raven had been the first beneficiary of her friends' husband-hunting zeal, having been introduced to Brent Radley in January. Brent was the sales manager at *Grasshopper*, the children's magazine Amanda published. Just yesterday Raven and Brent's brother, Hunter, four years her junior, had returned from their honeymoon in England. The road to marital bliss had contained a few speed bumps, but they all agreed it was results that counted.

The Wedding Ring was a closely guarded secret. The only outsiders who knew about it were Grandma Rossi and now Raven's new husband, Hunter Radley.

Charli had turned thirty last Wednesday, and her matchmaking buddies had lost no time setting her up with Grant Sterling, whom they'd described as mature, stable, affluent, gentlemanly, attractive—and perfect for Charli, who'd spent her entire adult life taking care of other people. She needed a strong, devoted husband, her friends had insisted—someone to take care of *her* for a change.

As much as she'd dreaded the almost inevitable rejection, the seductive thought just wouldn't let go: someone to take care of her. The kind of loving bond all seven of her siblings enjoyed with their spouses. Growing old with a man who adored her, surrounded by their children and grandchildren.

"What did you think of sushi?" Sunny asked. A strand of long, wavy auburn hair had worked itself free of her braid. She pushed it behind her ear.

"I liked it," Charli said. "Well, most of it."

"What did you think of sex?" Amanda asked.

Charli whipped her head around, praying none of her students had overheard.

Raven rolled her eyes. "Amanda..."

"You know nothing like that happened," Charli whispered. "It was our first date! And anyway, well, you know nothing like that happened."

She was, after all, Carlotta Rossi, last of a dying breed: the Thirty-Year-Old Virgin.

"No?" Amanda lifted her teacup. "I thought perhaps you'd asked your legal counsel to show you his, uh, briefs."

"Excuse me?" Jenny O'Keefe, one of the clarinets, caught Sunny's eye and lifted her coffee cup.

"Be right back," Sunny grumbled, and padded away in her white Reeboks.

"So you finally got to try sushi," Raven said. "Then what?"

Then Grant had wanted to deposit her back at home, Charli recalled. Only his good breeding had made him drag her to that club when her pride would have had her crawling back home at nine-thirty in the evening.

Thank goodness for good breeding, she thought with another little smile.

Raven was watching her closely. She squeezed Charli's hand. "You had a good time."

Charli took a deep breath. She nodded.

Amanda gave her an impatient little whack on the shoulder. "So where else did he take you?"

"To this club in the Twenties. Bunny's."

"Oh, I've been there. With Ben," Amanda said, referring to one of her two ex-husbands, a spendthrift and womanizing party animal.

"Well, I'd never been to a place like that." Charli had felt so intimidated, at first. Bunny's had been packed with people, all of them dressed in the latest hip fashions, acting so cool, totally at ease with the New York club scene.

"Who was performing?" Raven asked.

"Phil Rivera."

Charli's friends responded with wide-eyed "ooh"s.

Amanda asked, "Is he as hot in person as he is on MTV?"

"Hotter," Charli said, and they all erupted in girlish giggles. She leaned across the table, prompting Raven and Amanda to do the same. "I'd never been anyplace like that. It wasn't at all what I expected. The club was kind of small, and dark, and, well, it was a private show, by invitation. Grant did Rivera's divorce, and I guess they're on friendly terms now. Anyway, when we arrived, the man at the door, he checked Grant's name off on this list, just like in the movies."

Sunny returned. "What are you guys giggling about?"

They brought her up to speed on Charli's date.

"That is so cool!" Sunny declared.

"And then—" Charli raised her hands, signaling the pièce de résistance "—in the middle of his act, Rivera calls up a friend from the audience, to sing with him. Guess who! Skye Keiler!"

Her friends squealed in delight, drawing stares from the students. Skye Keiler was one of the biggest names in pop music.

"You saw Skye Keiler in person?" Raven said. "And Phil Rivera? Wow!"

"Grant introduced me to Rivera afterward. I shook hands with him and everything."

"So it was a good date," Raven said.

"It was—" Charli sighed "—wonderful."

Her friends exchanged knowing smiles.

"And Grant?" Sunny asked. "Was he wonderful?"

Charli's face hurt, she was grinning so widely. Never in her life had she felt this way.

Sunny laughed. She placed a hand on Charli's shoulder. "I think we have our answer."

Amanda leaned back in her seat. "Another Wedding Ring success story."

"Not yet!" Charli objected. "It was one date!"

"Did he kiss you good-night?" Sunny asked.

Charli thought she could probably fry an egg on her face, it felt so hot. "Yes," she said, so primly that her pals erupted in another fit of giggles.

At the club, Grant had plied her with scrumptious desserts, and coffee with amaretto liqueur when she'd declined anything stronger. He'd engaged her in conversation and gone out of his way to make sure she was comfortable, relaxed and entertained. By the time the first song had ended, she'd forgotten her wounded pride and her determination to rush home. They'd stayed at Bunny's for several hours, and Grant had been as sweetly attentive during the ride home as he'd been at the club.

And yes, he'd kissed her good-night, right there on her doorstep at two in the morning. He'd slid his hand around her neck, under her hair, and held her with such disarming gentleness that tears had pricked her eyes. She'd never been held like that, and certainly never kissed like that, lingeringly, savoringly, as if there were nowhere else he could possibly want to be, nothing else he could possibly want to do at that moment.

Charli had prepared for bed in a heady daze; it was

a wonder she'd managed to brush her teeth and wash that silly makeup off her face. Sleep had been elusive. She'd lain on her rickety little bed, staring into the dark, touching her lips. Remembering the kiss, the tender pressure of his mouth, the taste of him, more intoxicating than sake.

The evening had been so perfect—Grant had been so perfect—Charli shivered now, thinking about it.

Amanda yanked her out of her reverie. "When are you going to see him again?"

"I don't know." Soon, she hoped.

"Did he mention going out again?"

"Well, no."

A fleeting look passed among the other three. Charli's buoyant mood began to deflate. "Does that mean anything?"

"Probably not," Raven said, with a blasé shrug that didn't fool Charli for an instant.

The old familiar dejection pulled at her insides. "You're saying he's not going to call."

"Nobody's saying that." Raven touched Charli's arm. "Usually a man will say something about getting together again, but not always."

Sunny and Amanda murmured their agreement, but Charli could tell it was an act. She'd known these three since kindergarten.

"So if he doesn't call you," Amanda said, "you call him."

"I couldn't!"

"Why not?"

"I just couldn't badger him, if he doesn't want to see me."

"It's not badgering," Sunny said. "And I don't care what your parents might've told you. Or your grandma. Nowadays women ask men out all the time."

Charli slumped in her chair. She wasn't the type of modern woman who could call up a man for a date—especially if it was clear he wasn't interested.

What was that kiss, then—a gesture of mercy for the lonely, love-starved frump?

"Well, we just have to find Charli another man!" Amanda said. "No stuffy lawyers this time."

"Grant's not stuffy," Raven said. "He's an appealing guy, really genuine. I wouldn't have suggested him for Charli otherwise."

Sunny said, "He may seem genuine when he's stretched out on that recliner in your hypnotherapy office, telling you how traumatic it is to get a triple bogey on the eighteenth hole—"

"Oh, for pity's sake." Raven raked a hand through her chin-length, dark blond hair.

"—but if Charli says he's stuffy," Sunny continued, "he's stuffy."

"I never said he was stuffy," Charli murmured into her coffee. "It doesn't matter. I had fun, but—it isn't the end of the world if he doesn't call."

"We have to give Grant a chance," Raven said, "before we even think of finding someone else."

"Well, how much of a chance do we give him?" Amanda asked. "I mean, how long is Charli supposed to sit by the phone waiting for this guy to call?"

The image of her waiting by the phone was so pathetically apt, Charli wanted to cry.

"I want us to choose someone else now," Sunny said, "just, you know, as a backup."

"This discussion is premature." Raven skewered the other two with a pointed look.

"Fine," Sunny said, and squeezed Charli's shoulder. "All I'm going to say is that if this guy doesn't follow up, it's his loss."

Not if you took into account one minor detail.

Charli loved Grant Sterling.

3

GRANT STERLING LOVED GOLF.

He only wished it came easier to him. He watched Sam Kauffman flawlessly tee off, driving the ball two hundred yards onto the green, within putting distance of the sixth hole.

Grant had started playing golf only five years earlier, after joining Farman, Van Cleave and Holm. Once he'd realized that the fairways were where alliances were cemented and the occasional client wooed, he'd lost no time in learning the sport.

"Linda will meet us in the dining room at six," Sam said, referring to his wife. "You should've invited a date, made it a foursome."

"I like having my Sunday nights free," Grant said, as he withdrew his two iron from his golf bag. "Decompress a little before the workweek starts. Have a beer. Watch *X-Files*. Alone."

Sam laughed. "That doesn't sound bad. Linda usually picks Sunday nights for a bitch session. I get to hear about everything I did wrong all week."

"I'll remember that next time you get on my case about settling down."

"For a savvy guy, you can be a little dense about some things. I thought you wanted to make partner."

Grant stared off toward the distant flagstick, gauging the wind velocity, planning his shot. Sam had himself recently become a partner in Farman, Van Cleave and Holm. He was six years younger than Grant, but had joined the firm right out of law school.

This year, Grant thought. *It has to happen this year.* He refused to turn forty as an associate.

He'd made himself a promise nearly a quarter of a century ago, while squatting in a doorway overhang in downtown Philadelphia during a bitter March thunderstorm, scooping cold baked beans out of a tiny, single-serving can that he'd swiped from the nearby convenience store. He'd had to punch open the can with the rusty electrician's pocketknife he'd liberated days earlier from his old man's ratty work pants.

In his more vulnerable moments Grant could still feel the bone-rattling cold of that homeless night, not his first nor his last on the streets. He could still feel the panic that had grabbed his guts every time some other poor wretch made eye contact. He could still feel the raw welts on his back and taste those beans— Campbell's vegetarian style. If anything, his stomach had felt even emptier after he'd polished them off and wiped his fingers on his rain-soaked jeans.

That night sixteen-year-old Grant Sterling had made a promise to himself. He'd get as far away from his roots as humanly possible. He'd do whatever was necessary to put his brutal past behind him and build a life he could be proud of.

He'd never managed to expunge those first miserable sixteen years from his psyche—they were a part of him, like the color of his eyes and the lattice that decorated his back—but he'd come far in fulfilling that long-ago promise to himself. Becoming a partner in Farman, Van Cleave and Holm would be the crowning touch, a validation of his life and the sacrifices he'd made.

"You know the score with this firm," Sam persisted. "You knew it coming in."

"This has got to be the goddamn stuffiest bunch on Wall Street," Grant complained. "And the most hypocritical. Most of the senior partners are on their second marriage. Frank Van Cleave is paying alimony to two ex-Mrs. Van Cleaves. *Two*." He positioned the ball on the tee. "Yet he's got the nerve to lecture me about how marriage demonstrates character and stability."

"Hey, you're no longer in the D.A.'s office, Grant. This is Wall Street, the last stronghold of buttoned-down hypocrisy. The sad truth is, unless you want to retire as a senior associate, you'll have to learn to do things the Farman, Van Cleave way."

Translation: a tidy marriage to a suitable wife; the outward trappings of a balanced, well-adjusted personal life.

An unmarried associate, particularly one pushing forty, was viewed practically as an outsider, some sort of rogue elephant stomping all over the hallowed ideals upon which the firm had been founded. Such a rogue would never be fully welcomed into the herd, much less be considered "partner material."

And yes, Grant had known that going in, but he'd been convinced that once he'd proved himself, once he'd shown what a smart, hardworking attorney he was, that would be the only thing that mattered.

"I'm not the marrying type," Grant said, as he lined up his shot, concentrating on his overlapping grip, his wide stance, his even breathing.

"Are you the *partner* type?"

Grant sent his friend a baleful look. "I value my independence."

"So find some woman who doesn't mind you exercising your—" Sam waggled his brows salaciously "—independence."

"That's not what I meant." It was part of it, though. Grant enjoyed his sexual freedom. He liked dating a variety of women, never being tied down. He'd answered to no one but himself for the past twenty-three years, and he had no intention of relinquishing an iota of that hard-won autonomy.

He flexed into his backswing, his downswing, felt his weight shift easily into his follow-through as the club snapped the ball and sent it flying. He watched it arc to the left and drop neatly into one of two twin sand traps in front of the green.

"Ever think of trying your three wood?" Sam asked.

Only the last few times you suggested it, Grant thought, irritated by the unsolicited advice, which he knew would probably prove to be on target if he weren't too proud and stubborn to heed it. Like many of their colleagues, Sam had spent his youth diligently perfecting his swing while Grant had been busing tables and scrubbing pots—at this very country club—for minimum wage.

He and Sam started down the fairway, towing the handcarts holding their golf bags. At thirty-nine, Grant had to admit he'd never be another Jack Nicklaus. Nevertheless, he was confident that with enough practice, he'd at least become a competent player. Compared to other challenges he'd overcome, this was nothing.

That was something Raven Muldoon, his hypnotherapist, had helped him put in perspective. He'd been on his own since he was a teenager, she'd reminded him, supporting himself at odd jobs once he'd made his way to Long Island, working himself into exhaustion while finishing high school. Then it had been a mad scramble for work-study programs, the occasional scholarship and low-interest student loan, so he could earn his B.A. at Queens College and his law degree at New York University. The payoff was a rewarding, if sometimes frustrating, legal career approaching the fifteen-year mark.

Raven was right. If he could accomplish all that, after his ignoble start in life, he could learn to hit a little dimpled ball into a hole without going several strokes over par.

Raven had been right about that, but she'd been dead wrong about his taste in women. Charli Rossi wasn't his type. He preferred sophisticated, experienced women. Women who knew the score and wanted the same thing from him that he wanted from them: stimulating companionship and no-strings-attached sex. These women knew *maki* from sashimi. They knew how to keep up their side of an animated conversation. They knew how to dress.

Was that dowdy frock the best Charli could come up with? And the cardigan. Good God. With that plain hairstyle and those serviceable pumps, she looked like a librarian from Central Casting. She'd worn a little makeup, but obviously wasn't used to it; she'd rubbed her eyes a couple of times, leaving mascara smears under them. They were her best feature, her eyes, a brown so dark they were nearly black.

As for the rest of her, well, there wasn't much about her he could call alluring, much less arousing.

Except when he'd glanced across the table and caught her wriggling out of that awful sweater. Perhaps it was the artlessness of the movement, the fact that she was clearly oblivious to the way the material of her dress stretched over breasts that seemed suddenly much more lush and full than they had a moment before.

He smiled at the recollection. Sneaky breasts. A pleasant surprise. She'd done a little shimmy while working the sleeves off her arms. Grant had schooled his expression—second nature after all his years as a lawyer—but for one startling heartbeat of time she'd managed to push his buttons. Without even realizing it.

But that was a few seconds out of a five-hour date. On the whole, Charli Rossi didn't do it for him—although he couldn't deny there was something endearing about her. He'd be lying if he claimed he hadn't enjoyed watching her experience new things. The sushi, for one. She'd surprised him. He'd expected to see her react with distaste, or at best try one or two polite bites and leave the rest. Instead she'd eagerly polished off half of that large platter.

And no one had to tell him that last night had been her first club experience. Her wide-eyed fascination was almost comical. By then Grant's nagging conscience had kicked in and he'd decided he owed her a good time. He'd bet anything she wasn't accustomed to going out on the town, and he'd done his best to put her at ease, to make this date everything she expected a proper date to be, right down to the good-night kiss.

Grant frowned, recalling that kiss. He'd initiated it because he'd known she'd expected it, or at least hoped for it. Didn't every real date end with a kiss? What had started out as a friendly peck had turned into another surprise.

Instead of the awkward stiffness he'd anticipated, she'd been soft and warm and shyly responsive—a result of the sake she'd consumed, no doubt, but at that moment he hadn't stopped to reason it out. Masculine instinct had taken over and he'd let his lips tarry, savoring the moment and the thrill of awareness, as fleeting as it was unexpected.

On retrospect, the kiss had been a mistake. Grant didn't make a habit of planting false expectations.

He hoped Charli wouldn't be too disappointed when she didn't hear from him again.

Grant grabbed his sand wedge and shuffled into the downward-sloping sand trap. Though he was used to it by now, he hated having his opponent cool his heels while he extricated his ball from whatever unfortunate location it had found its way to. He especially hated it when he was playing against a senior partner or an important client. In this case it was just Sam Kauffman, a junior partner he'd gotten chummy with over the past five years, but it still rankled. He'd never beaten Sam.

Although the hypnosis sessions with Raven had been helping Grant focus on his game, today was shaping up as a washout. He felt distracted. His first ball had ended up in a water hazard. His fourth had landed in the rough, and he'd had a hell of a time hitting it out of the dense shrubbery.

"Dig your feet into the sand," Sam called down to him.

Twelve more holes to go, and Grant found he was no longer looking forward to them. He ground his shoes into the sand and calculated what it would take to pop the ball up to the green, which was at shoulder height. Focusing intently, he swung, hit with a spray of sand, started to smile—

And watched the damn thing plop into the opposite sand trap. He cursed.

Sam turned back to him. "You should've hit behind the ball."

What the hell do you think I was trying to do? Grant made his way out of the sand trap and across the fringe to the other one.

"Slow down on your backswing," Sam advised. He squinted toward the green, where his own ball waited for him, not five yards from the hole. Grant saw him sneak a peek at his Breitling sport watch.

Charli had caught Grant doing the same thing last night, and he found he didn't like it any better than she had. Only she hadn't gotten irritated—not that he could tell, anyway. She'd held her chin high and pretended she was as eager to end the date as he was.

He hadn't expected that, for some reason—that balky pride. It wasn't the first time some guy had cut the evening short, he'd realized then. She was all too used to it.

She may have been used to it, but the pain was there, lurking behind those inky-dark eyes. That was when he'd blurted that out about taking her to Bunny's. Which had been part of his original plan, of course, before he'd set eyes on his mousy blind date, at which point those plans had abruptly changed.

In the end, he'd practically had to hog-tie Charli to get her to that club, once she'd made up her mind to help him burn her off.

Grant had the feeling he'd met his match in the stubborn-pride department.

Concentrate. He eyeballed the height of the green, the position of the ball. He consciously paused—*the hell with Sam, let him wait*—while he replayed Raven's words in his mind, her techniques for mentally zooming in on a task, to the exclusion of all else. He took a slow, deep breath, focused on the ball and on his body, as if they were somehow connected. He felt it gel, come together just right.

He knew the shot was good even before he watched the ball bounce once and stop ten feet from the hole. He took a few moments to smooth the sand traps with the rake kept there for that purpose. His shoes were filled with sand; it littered both sides of the green, a testament to his skill level.

Sam dropped his fifteen-foot birdie putt effortlessly. Grant was already one over par, and he only made it worse when he skirted the hole on his first putt, putting the ball four feet past it.

"Son of a bitch," he muttered under his breath. Sam

must have sensed his mood, because for once he held his tongue. Grant forced himself to relax and concentrate. A double bogey was bad enough; he had no intention of making it worse.

He tapped the ball and it rolled slowly toward the hole, flirted with the rim—Grant held his breath—and finally teetered into it.

"Your problem," Sam said, "is those women you date."

Grant retrieved his ball. "I thought you were going to say it's my backswing."

"You go for these outspoken, independent types. They're no more ready to tie the knot than you are. And even if they were, they're not the kind of wife you need. What you need is some sweet, sheltered young thing with a strong regard for family. What?" Sam asked, studying Grant's expression. "You know someone like that?"

"Sure." Grant slid his putter into his golf bag. "I took her out just last night."

"Yeah, right," Sam scoffed. "I'm serious, Grant. Women like that still exist—you just have to know where to look for them."

"In a convent?" They took off together toward the seventh tee.

"You need a dependable woman with traditional values," Sam said. "A woman who doesn't feel she has to always put herself first."

"Mother Teresa is no longer with us, Sam."

"Would you get off this nun thing? I'm talking about a woman who knows how to be a team player."

"The 'Grant Sterling for Partner' team."

"Okay, yes! Because it's to *her* benefit as much as yours if you make partner. Teamwork. You see what I'm getting at?"

"This paragon should be quiet and unassuming, I take it. One might even say mousy. The kind of woman who, at thirty years of age, still lives with her folks."

"Go ahead, joke. It's *your* career."

"It would help, of course," Grant continued, "if she possessed impeccable housekeeping and organizational skills. And if she were adept at entertaining my business colleagues. The kind of woman who would think nothing of, say, whipping up a five-course dinner for eighty. Plus a cake."

Sam gave a disgusted sigh. "Forget I said anything."

I wish I could.

4

"CHARLI, HOW ARE YOU? It's Grant."

Something snagged hard in Charli's chest, knocking her off balance. She slid into a kitchen chair, keeping a death grip on the receiver of the wall phone.

He wasn't going to call; she'd reconciled herself to it. Her friends had tried to prepare her—

"You there?" he asked.

"Oh, I'm sorry, I...hi."

Mama screeched down the stairs, "Who is it, Carlotta?"

Charli covered the mouthpiece and called, "It's—it's for me."

"Tell her not to call so late!" Mama hollered, obviously assuming the caller was one of Charli's female friends.

"Did I call too late?" Grant asked.

"No, no. Don't worry about it. Mama goes to bed early, but she lies there watching the Weather Channel for a couple of hours. She just doesn't believe anyone else should have a life after 9:00 p.m."

Grant's rich chuckle brought a smile to Charli's face. "I wanted you to know how much I enjoyed last night," he said.

Her smile spread into a moronic grin. That funny

feeling in her chest turned into a swelling warmth. "Me, too. I had a wonderful time, Grant."

"I was hoping we could do it again soon. Actually, I had something a little different in mind. The opening of an exhibit at a photo gallery in SoHo."

"Another client?"

"The daughter of one of the partners at my firm. She's an accomplished photographer. I think you'll enjoy her work."

"I'd love to."

"Are you free Wednesday night?"

A wave of embarrassment washed over Charli. She'd accepted without even knowing what day he was talking about. "Yes, I...Wednesday's good."

"Terrific!" he said, as if he really meant it. "I'll pick you up at seven, if that's okay. We'll get a bite to eat after." An impish tone infected his voice as he added, "You can choose the restaurant this time."

"Oh, wherever you want to go is fine!" she blurted.

"You know what I'd really like? A good Italian meal. I'll bet you know your way around Little Italy."

"Oh, I know a wonderful restaurant in Little Italy! The best *ossobuco* in the city."

"I can't wait. See you Wednesday. Good night, Charli."

"Good night."

Charli replaced the receiver on the wall phone, then snatched it up immediately and dialed Raven's number.

"IS THIS A NEW PIECE?" Charli examined the antique metal weather vane, in the shape of a galleon under full sail. It occupied a space on Grant's white fireplace mantel between a painted wooden statue of a black-and-white pony that dated from the 1830s, and a primitive painting of a New England farm scene.

"I found that at a flea market on Saturday. It was made in the late eighteen hundreds." Grant reclined in the corner of his L-shaped beige suede sofa, with one leg stretched out on the cushions and both arms thrown over the sofa back. Lazily he lifted one hand and beckoned to Charli.

She recognized that inviting smile, and answered it with a shy one of her own. During the two weeks they'd been seeing each other, she'd come to relish Grant's kisses and warm caresses, although she was careful to hide her eagerness. She didn't want him to think she was, well, eager. Brazen. A wanton woman. She'd die of shame if he thought of her like that.

Charli crossed the wide oak floorboards, partially covered by a painted canvas floor covering in an oak-leaf pattern that reflected the warm autumn tones Grant favored. Like the rest of his three-story water-front house on Long Island's North Shore, the living room was sophisticated yet cozy, home to the eclectic assortment of American folk art he'd collected over the years.

The stone-and-shingle exterior, too, was a pleasing study in contrasts. The brown and gray granite blocks of the first floor were set off by white Tuscan-style columns, while towering granite chimneys bisected the cedar-clad gables flanking the recessed front entrance.

During the day the living room's sprawling bay window gave a breathtaking view of Long Island

Sound. It was now around nine at night, and Roman shades of a soft cream-and-beige fabric draped the windows. A table lamp with an amber-colored mica shade cast soft light over Grant, who watched her approach and sit next to him, close but not touching.

His fingers slipped under her hair to lightly stroke her neck. Charli shivered at the pleasurable sensation. He exerted gentle pressure, urging her to lean against him, and she did. She'd never felt this with any of the handful of men she'd dated, this easy companionship, as if the two of them "fit" somehow.

"Do you mind that we didn't do more this evening?" he asked.

"No, of course not! Sometimes it's nice to just...cuddle," she admitted, settling more fully against him as his arm draped over her shoulder.

After work he'd changed into a wine-colored polo shirt and khaki slacks, and picked her up for a casual dinner at a deli-style restaurant that had been a fixture in her neighborhood since before she was born. They'd bought dessert—gourmet ice-cream bars—on the way to his house.

Charli and Grant had seen each other nearly every day for the past two weeks. She'd even invited him to Easter dinner yesterday, expecting him to politely decline. After all, for a man to willingly spend time with a girlfriend's family, he had to be pretty serious about her, or so she'd been told.

Not only had Grant shown up, but he'd brought Mama a hostess gift of potted lilies, plus a bottle of good Italian wine. He'd complimented the food and flattered Grandma Rossi, and after dinner, while the women had tidied the kitchen, he'd sat in the living room with Papa, tossing back sambuca and speculating on the Yankees' chances of bringing home the pennant this year.

Tonight Charli had pulled back the top and sides of her hair with a white bow barrette fastened in back. The hardware poked her scalp where Grant's shoulder cradled her head, prompting her to unfasten the barrette and set it on the hammered-copper coffee table. Tossing her hair off her face, she snuggled back against him, only to have him tip up her head and stare at her.

She brought her hand to her face. "What?"

He brushed his fingertips through her loosened hair, slowly.

"Oh, I'm a mess," Charli said, wishing she'd left the barrette in place.

"No, you look lovely this way." His gaze took in her hair, her eyes, her mouth. "Natural."

"I'm not lovely." Charli tried to pull back, but he wouldn't let her. "You don't have to say things like that, Grant. I know I'm not... You don't have to say things like that."

He searched her eyes, and Charli got that uncomfortable feeling again, that he saw more than she wanted him to.

Finally he said, "There's nothing wrong with the way you look, Charli."

She forced a chuckle. "Nothing that a nose job wouldn't fix. For starters."

His brows quirked as if he couldn't decide whether she was joking. "What's wrong with your nose?"

She let her snort of laughter answer him.

He held her chin, studying her. "It's not a tiny little turned-up nose, I'll give you that."

"Your powers of observation are exemplary."

He turned her head for the full profile. "But it's no beak, either. Does it really bother you?"

"Grant, it's..." She touched the nose she'd always thought of as, yes, a beak. "It—it overpowers my face."

"It's a strong nose, and I like it." He made her face him, his gaze as candid as she'd ever seen it. "Your nose suits you, Charli, and it doesn't overpower your face. I wouldn't say it if it weren't true."

He wasn't calling her ravishing, he wasn't comparing her to the world's great beauties—she never would have bought that nonsense for a second. He was simply telling her he liked her nose, and his unblinking sincerity brought grateful tears to her eyes. She tucked her head into his shoulder and struggled for composure.

Tenderly he held her, kissed the top of her head. After a few moments he added, "But as for these Dumbo ears..." and he tugged on her earlobe.

Charli laughed. Her ears were perfectly formed, the only part of her she had no problem with. His gaze homed in on her mouth, and she knew he was going to kiss her. Her heart sprinted as he lowered his head and touched his lips to hers.

As always, it was a little shock, the pleasure of it, and she nearly groaned aloud. It was as if his mouth were making love to hers—not that she had experience in that area, but she had an imagination, and her imagination filled in the blanks. He kissed her with increasing fervor, and by the time his tongue stroked her lips and slipped past them, she welcomed the bold invasion.

Grant had kissed Charli like this before, and it excited her, but she always restrained the impulse to respond in kind, unsure what he expected of her, wary of being labeled a certain kind of woman. Without warning, he lifted her onto his lap, gentling her with whispered endearments when she tensed. He pulled her legs up onto the cushions and leaned her comfortably against the plush sofa back, the two of them now tucked cozily into the corner.

He nuzzled her throat above the V-collar of her pink-and-white awning-striped blouse. "What kind of perfume is that? You always smell so good."

"Dove soap," she said, and felt him smile against her neck.

"I'll buy you a case." He kissed the patch of skin showing under the hollow of her throat, and claimed her lips again as his hand slid over her breast.

He'd tried to touch her like that a couple of times before, and those times she'd silently blocked his hand. Now, however, she sat still as stone, and after a couple of moments, his long fingers began to move.

Grant lifted his head and watched her face as he gently kneaded her breast, right through her blouse and bra. She turned her head aside, unable to look him in the eye, afraid to let him see how his touch affected her. Every nerve in her body hummed. She'd fantasized during the past two weeks, wondering how it would feel to have him touch her there, and other places as well. If this was how it felt over her clothes—this delicious tingling warmth—how would it feel on bare skin?

Charli had always been self-conscious about her breasts, which she considered a bit too large for her short frame, though she'd learned how to dress to minimize them. Now, as Grant stroked and caressed them, that insecurity came rushing to the fore. Suddenly, despite the raw pleasure of his touch, she wanted him to stop.

He must have sensed it, because his hand moved from there to her side, and then lower, skimming her waist, settling on her hip. He pulled her closer, kissed her with an intensity that stole her wits. He stroked her hip and thigh through her navy twill skirt, and Charli ached to touch him, too, to cling to him, to give in to the mounting urge to move against him—but she didn't dare. These feelings were so new, at once welcome and unnerving, and she didn't trust herself to respond in the appropriate manner—whatever could be considered "appropriate" when you were perched on a man's lap letting him touch you where you'd never been touched!

Grant broke the kiss. He let his gaze travel down her form and up again, as if appreciating the way she looked sprawled on his lap. Her hair was now thoroughly disheveled, and she wished for a comb, until she noticed the heated look in his eyes.

"If you'd looked like this when I picked you up," he said, as he arranged the tousled strands around her face, "I would've brought you back here right away, and to hell with dinner."

His fingers went to the top button of her blouse. He flicked it free of the buttonhole and reached for the second one. Charli stayed his hands.

"It's all right," he murmured. His warm knuckles grazed the skin he'd exposed, and the edge of her white cotton bra. "I've got protection."

Charli swallowed hard, beset by conflicting impulses. She knew what he meant by protection—she wasn't *that* naive! Nor was she so naive that she failed to identify the rigid shape nudging her through his pants. This man wanted to make love to her, this man she loved, this man she'd lain awake fantasizing about for the past two weeks.

Never in Charli's life had her principles been so sorely tested. She knew she was hopelessly old-fashioned by current standards, but to her, sex and marriage went hand in hand. After all, it was the most intimate act two people could share. The bottom line was, if she loved a man enough to take that ultimate step, she loved him enough to marry him. She'd long ago reconciled herself to the fact that she wasn't likely to experience either in her lifetime.

Men, of course, rarely saved themselves for marriage. Grant was no doubt accustomed to casual intimacy; he'd probably been having sex since he was a teenager. Lord knew how many women had shared his bed. To him Charli might represent nothing more than another notch in his belt. A convenient body.

Her voice was a ragged whisper as she fumbled with her buttons. "I don't want to."

Her refusal came as no surprise to Grant, she could

tell. Still, he said, with a little smile, "If you give me half a chance, I could make you want to."

You already have.

She didn't say it, though, and after a moment he patted her arm and said, "I won't press you, Charli. Perhaps it's just as well."

She puzzled over that as he set her off his lap. Was he agreeing with her that it was too soon, or did he feel it was just as well that they didn't make love because they had no future together?

Grant's mood seemed to swing 180 degrees in the time it took him to come to his feet. Mere seconds ago he'd been relaxed, amorous, even playful. Now he seemed suddenly subdued, preoccupied.

This is it, she thought. *He's going to tell me it's over. He's trying to decide how to break the news.*

"Would you wait here a second?" he asked, somewhat formally.

"Of course."

Grant left the living room. Charli sat stiffly on the edge of the sofa, staring at the cluster of antique game boards propped on a picture rail across the room. Listening to a distant ship's horn on the Sound. Preparing herself for the worst.

You knew it couldn't last forever. At least you'll have wonderful memories.

What was he doing? Perhaps she'd left something here and he wanted to give it to her before he showed her the door.

The sound of approaching footfalls shoved her heart into her throat. She'd break it off herself, Charli decided. Before he had the chance.

Then she remembered. The Wedding Ring pact. She couldn't call it quits for three months, as long as Grant was still interested. And if he wasn't, well, then he had to be the one to do the breaking up. She wasn't allowed to salvage her pride by beating him to the punch.

To Charli, the Wedding Ring pact was a solemn promise; the rules she and her friends had agreed to were not to be taken lightly. So she had no choice but to sit there and take whatever humiliation was in store for her.

"Sorry to keep you waiting," Grant said, as he reentered the room. His expression now unreadable, he sat next to her and touched her eyelids. "Close your eyes."

She did as he asked. He lifted her left hand. She felt something hard and cool slide over the tip of her third finger and settle snugly at the base.

She stopped breathing.

"Open your eyes, Charli."

She found herself staring at a large solitaire diamond set in a wide, satin-finished platinum band and surrounded by an irregular scattering of smaller, flush-mounted diamonds. It looked like the sun among a handful of fallen stars.

Grant said, "Will you marry me?"

5

"Open your eyes, Charli. Please."

The voice penetrated her consciousness first, followed by the feel of the suede upholstery beneath her, and warm, strong hands rubbing hers. It was Grant's voice, but she'd never heard him sound so rattled.

Charli opened her eyes. She was lying on Grant's sofa. Her feet were elevated on a toast-colored, chenille pillow. His worried face stared down at her.

"Thank God," he said, and offered a shaky smile. "You go in for high drama, I see. Does passing out cold mean yes or no?"

"What?" Then she remembered.

The ring. *Will you marry me?*

Groggily she lifted her hand. The exquisite ring was still there. "I *fainted?*" She started to sit up.

Grant firmly pressed her back down. "Don't try to get up just yet. Give it a few minutes. How are you feeling?"

"Fine. I just...I guess it was a shock."

He gave her that tender little smile, the one she loved to see. "Well, I'd say you evened the score."

"You asked me to marry you," Charli murmured, incredulous.

"I know we've only known each other a very short time, but...I consider myself a better than average judge of people, Charli. I don't need more time to know that you and I are a good match."

"You don't think we should wait awhile, get better acquainted?"

"Everything that's important, we already know about each other. We have a lifetime to sort out the small stuff. All I know is I've found the right woman. And at thirty-nine, I don't feel like waiting around another year or two when we could get married now and get on with our lives."

Charli smiled as tears of joy clogged her throat. She was the right woman. He'd said so. And he was impatient to make her his.

He lifted her hand and stared at the engagement ring he'd placed on it. "You probably think I'm crazy for proposing so soon after Raven introduced us."

"Not really," she said. "In my family, arranged marriages are the norm—at least they were until my generation. Nonni didn't choose her husband, but they were devoted to each other for sixty years, even though they met only once or twice before the wedding. And my parents—you may not think they're such a happy couple, the way they carp at each other all the time, but they really love each other. And that was a short engagement, too, arranged by my grandparents." She smiled. "They didn't believe in waiting too long—no point giving the young people time to get up to mischief before the wedding."

She'd expected Grant to share her droll smile, but for some reason, her words had a sobering effect on him. "We need to get a couple of things clear from the start," he said. "Before you give me your answer."

Charli sat up, with his assistance. She tried to finger-comb her hair, but it was hopelessly snarled. The ring snagged a strand of hair, and she gazed at it once more, turning it this way and that, watching bursts of light detonate in the stones. She wasn't used to wearing rings, but she knew she'd have no trouble getting used to this one. Never in her life had she owned anything like this. She'd only seen this kind of jewelry in magazine ads.

"As I said," Grant continued, "I'm pushing forty. I've worked hard for many years to orchestrate the kind of life that suits me—from where I live to what I do for a living to who I spend my time with. I guess you could say I'm set in my ways. And I'm sure in certain respects, you are, too."

"Well, I guess so." Charli wanted to tell him she was thrilled at the prospect of drastic change in her life, but it didn't seem to be what he wanted to hear just then. She supposed all men faced marriage with some degree of trepidation, particularly men who'd been living on their own as long as Grant had.

"There are different kinds of marriages," Grant said. "Each with its own set of...expectations. You must know what I mean."

"Well, sure. Every couple is unique, after all."

"Precisely. The kind of marriage I'm proposing will be somewhat different from the norm. You and I won't, uh..." He made vague hand gestures, obviously grappling for the right words. "What I mean is, this will be a...companionable union. A mutually advantageous, um, partnership based on respect for each other's autonomy."

Charli bit her lip, stifling a giggle. He sounded so lawyerly, so formal and ill at ease, so at odds with the easy familiarity she'd come to expect from him. He must be really nervous.

"My current lifestyle," Grant added, "will remain unchanged." He was looking over her shoulder rather than directly at her.

"I understand," she said, privately amused at his reference to maintaining his elegant lifestyle. As if there could be any question that he'd be a good provider!

He glanced at her, and away. "This is a little awkward, but...I'm accustomed to enjoying a, um, what could be called an active social life. That won't stop when I get married."

Charli wouldn't ask that of him. The last thing she wanted was to turn into the kind of harridan who begrudged her husband the occasional fishing trip or night out with the boys.

"I know how to be discreet, Charli. I'll do nothing to bring shame on you. Considering the sort of expedient, um, practical marriage we're talking about," he said, "there's no reason I shouldn't pursue my own, uh...that is, it's not as if you and I will even be..."

Charli couldn't believe it— Grant was blushing!

She laid her hand over his, wanting nothing more than to put him out of his misery. "We're not a couple of twenty-year-old kids entering into a marriage that's all passion and no practicality. I want the same things you do, Grant." She squeezed his hand. "And don't worry—I respect your independence. I'm not going to turn into your warden."

"Does that mean your answer is yes?"

"Of course it's yes!" she said with a laugh. On impulse she threw her arms around his neck and kissed him—the first time she'd initiated a kiss.

Grant seemed surprised, but only for a second. He kissed her back and said, "This is going to work, Charli. I know it is."

"Of course it's going to work!" *Because we're in love*, she thought, but didn't say it. She could only speak for herself, and she couldn't bring herself to declare her love before he did.

Perhaps Grant didn't love her yet, not the way she loved him, and that was okay. Grandpa Rossi hadn't loved Nonni when he'd spoken his vows; their deep feelings had grown over time. And Mama had confided that it had been that way with her and Papa, too.

Grant was right: everything that was important, they already knew about each other. During the past two weeks she'd learned that beneath the polite reserve, Grant Sterling was a man of passion and warmth. She sensed a profound, unshakable connection between the two of them. Yes, their love would blossom and grow in time.

Resolutely she ignored the nagging inner voice that warned this was much too sudden, that her bridegroom's vision of wedded bliss needed greater scrutiny. If she challenged him, she might scare him off, and then what did she have to look forward to? Living out her life as a lonely old maid in the house she'd grown up in, seeing to everyone's happiness but her own.

Grant said, "You should know there's a good chance I'll make partner this year."

From the way he said this, Charli could tell it meant a great deal to him. "Good luck," she said. "I wish there were some way I could help make it happen."

His smile faltered. He held her gaze for long moments, and she could tell something troubled him. She was about to ask him about it, but just then he touched her cheek—a fleeting brush of his fingers—and said, "Let's go give your folks the good news."

6

CHARLI HAD NEVER WORN anything like the frilly white negligee she'd just slipped into, a chiffon-and-lace concoction that Raven had helped her pick out. She'd declined Amanda's offer to help her shop for a last-minute trousseau. She loved Amanda dearly, but didn't dare come to her husband's bed in the kind of indecent nightie she knew Amanda favored.

Charli examined her reflection in the full-length standing cheval mirror that occupied a corner of the guest room in Grant's house, where he'd left her suitcase. He must have known she'd appreciate a private place to get ready for their first night together.

The gown's snug stretch-lace bodice and thin double spaghetti straps accentuated her full bosom and displayed more cleavage than anything she'd worn in her life. And she could even make out— Charli peered closely at the mirror. Yes! She could see her nipples! Just the barest shadow through the filmy cloth, but there they were! Reflexively she snatched up the matching robe, as sheer and feminine as the gown, and put it on. She pulled it closed, turning this way and that to check for see-through.

She stopped abruptly. This was ridiculous. In a short while her new husband would see all of her.

What difference did it make if her nightgown provided a sneak preview? Wasn't that kind of the point?

She bit her lip, stifling a gust of nervous laughter, and threw off the robe. Taking a deep breath, she placed her palm over her thumping heart. "This is it, Carlotta," she told her reflection. "Are you ready?"

Less than a week had passed since Grant's hasty proposal. It was now around midnight, and the last of their guests had just departed. Charli and Grant had spoken their vows that afternoon in Grant's living room—*their* living room now—before a justice of the peace. She'd worn a silk dress in pale apricot, with a matching jacket. Raven had helped her shop for that, too.

The wedding band Grant had placed on her finger matched the engagement ring. It was made of the same satin-finished platinum, set with more of the starlike, flush-mounted diamonds. It had been a single-ring ceremony. Grant didn't care for rings, he'd said. It shouldn't have irked Charli—after all, he was legally married, ring or no ring. Still, she would have been so happy and proud to slip a gleaming wedding band on her husband's finger.

The honeymoon was another disappointment. It would have to wait until the summer, when Grant had scheduled a vacation. Right now he was handling several cases and couldn't afford the time.

The ceremony had been followed by a buffet dinner, also at the house. Grant had insisted on the small, private, civil ceremony, much to the horror of Charli's parents, who felt that only a formal church wedding with a priest officiating had God's seal of approval.

In truth, Charli had always dreamed of a huge church wedding with an elaborate reception. Her fantasies had included a full-skirted white wedding gown and a bevy of bridesmaids. She'd lobbied for a delay of several weeks so she could plan a real wedding, but Grant's mind had been made up and so she'd backed off, wary of rocking the boat. Thus only a handful of his pals had witnessed their vows, plus her own closest friends and jumbo-size family. Her new husband, she'd learned, was estranged from his parents and had no siblings.

Charli, however, had siblings enough for the both of them. As soon as she'd accepted Grant's proposal, she'd called an emergency family meeting to devise a plan for taking care of their parents and grandmother. Charli's sisters and brothers had always claimed they were too busy to offer assistance, although she'd noticed they managed to make time for cooking classes and bowling leagues and craft clubs and trips to Atlantic City and shopping jaunts to Manhattan and PTA bake sales and Little League coaching, just for starters.

She'd put some long-overdue starch in her backbone and informed them all that they were going to start pulling their weight. Most of them whined and moaned, but in the end she'd managed to hammer out a weekly schedule acceptable to everyone. For once in her life, Charli Rossi had asserted herself; she'd refused to take no for an answer.

And it had felt darn good!

Charli removed her pearl-studded hair clip, recalling Grant's reaction when she'd let down her hair last week. He'd called her lovely. No man had ever said that to her, or anything like it. She leaned forward, shook out her hair and tossed it back.

And gaped at the results. Between the alluring gown and the windblown hair and the glitter of anticipation in her eyes, she almost didn't recognize herself.

Leaving her robe on the carpet where it had fallen, Charli crossed to the door and stood with her fingers on the knob, listening intently. Had Grant come upstairs yet? Was he waiting for her in his room? *Their* room, she reminded herself.

She let herself out and padded down the hall to the next door. Taking a deep breath, she knocked gently. No answer. Muted sounds came from downstairs—Grant walking around, no doubt locking up the house. She slipped into the room and closed the door, flicking on the wall switch to light the pair of antique, glass-shaded bedside lamps.

The bedroom was decorated in the same earthy hues as the rest of the house, but in darker, richer tones, with black accents. It was a man's room, and definitely a man's bed, wide and imposing, the towering headboard and squat footboard covered in padded tan leather. The bedspread was box-quilted black velour, the sheets and pillowcases fine black linen.

Slowly Charli approached the bed, feeling like an interloper in this unapologetically masculine space. Her things would be moved here from her parents' house tomorrow. Perhaps when she saw her dresses hanging in the closet next to Grant's suits, her hairbrush and jewelry box on the dresser top along with his cuff links and collar stays, she'd begin to feel as if she belonged here.

The contrasting textures of leather, velour and linen drew her fingers. Tentatively she stroked the pillowcase, as smooth and inviting as silk.

This was where it would happen. Tonight. The man she loved would bare her and touch her and bind his body with hers. He'd do what he'd wanted to do last week—what she'd wanted, too, if she was being honest. What she'd made herself half-mad thinking about in the intervening days and nights. Never in her life had she felt as womanly, as desired, as *sexual,* as she had these last few days, waiting for her wedding night.

Charli sat on the edge of the bed. She bounced a little, testing the firmness of the mattress. That brought to mind the serious bouncing this mattress would get tonight, and she clamped her hand over the chortle that erupted. Sliding into the center of the bed, she sat cross-legged and arranged her diaphanous white gown around herself, marveling at how stark it looked against the black spread.

She tugged the deep V neckline of her gown up a little. She jerked it back down again. And waited.

Less than a minute later the doorknob turned. Charli's heart gave her a one-two punch as she greeted her husband with a shy smile.

Grant stopped dead in his tracks, staring at his wife, his fingers frozen in the act of loosening his necktie. "Charli. What are you doing here?"

Her smile withered. The one-two punch in her chest turned into a giant fist, squeezing.

He started to speak, and stopped, clearly disconcerted. He pulled his necktie free and tossed it and his dark blue suit coat over a chair back. His gaze swept over her, as if seeking the answer to his question, though he'd already figured it out; she could see it in his eyes.

"Charli..." His expression was baffled, dismayed. He took one step toward her, then stopped. "We talked about this," he said quietly.

Charli clutched handfuls of chiffon in her lap. Her voice was so small, she barely heard herself. "What do you mean?"

"This was all settled. The kind of marriage this will be."

"The kind of—" Charli swallowed around a hard lump. "You mean you don't want to...?" She looked at the bed she sat on.

He stalked a few steps away, scrubbing at his nape. "I know I went over all this." His gaze turned inward, as if he was replaying the conversation in his mind.

"I don't... When?" She tried to yank her neckline up, drawing Grant's eyes. He looked away quickly.

"Last week," he said, "when I proposed."

"You didn't say we wouldn't..."

"Yes I did. And you said it was what you wanted, too. A companionable marriage."

Companionable. She remembered him using that word, and others. Such as *expedient* and...

"Practical," she said dully. "That's what you meant."

Would a more sophisticated woman, the kind of worldly woman Grant was accustomed to, have understood that he was talking about a platonic marriage?

Charli hugged her chiffon-draped knees to her chest. "Why?" she whispered, damming up the tears through sheer force of will.

He sighed. "If you'd seen what I've seen working on divorce cases, you wouldn't ask that. The tearful recriminations. Vicious custody battles. Spouses who once vowed their undying love doing everything possible to destroy each other. I've seen plenty of my own friends go through that hell, too."

Charli struggled to follow his reasoning. "But what does that have to do with...?"

"Most marriages are based on roller-coaster emotions, starting with the raging desire that brought the couple together in the first place. No two people can sustain that kind of passion over the long haul, or the starry-eyed love they started out with. When the inevitable disillusionment sets in, people tend to turn all that fire and fury against the very person they swore they'd love till death did them part."

Something about this didn't add up. Yes, marriages failed. Spouses turned against each other. It happened all too often. Yet even in the face of grim divorce statistics, plenty of people—including divorce lawyers—still fell in love every day, still offered up their hearts unreservedly. It was human nature to hope, to dream, to commit oneself to a mate, to foresee a future of promise and fulfillment, not disillusionment and pain.

There had to be something else behind Grant's bleak vision of marriage, something he wasn't telling her. It struck Charli then just how little she knew about the man she'd promised to honor and cherish for the rest of her life.

"But you wanted to...you know." She hugged herself tighter. "Last week."

He gave her a wry half smile. "Men are simple creatures, Charli. Opportunistic even. We don't need much in the way of inducement when it comes to sex."

A scalding wave of shame suffused Charli. To Grant she had indeed been nothing more than a convenient body—and not a particularly enticing one at that. Not much in the way of inducement, according to her new husband.

Grant continued, "I could tell you didn't welcome my advances. I took that to be a sign that this kind of arrangement would suit you. You needn't be concerned that I'll make those kinds of demands on you. That's why I gave you the guest room."

Not as a changing room for her wedding night, she now realized, but as a permanent separate bedroom. He thought she was uninterested in sex. There was a nasty word men applied to such women: *frigid.* That was how her husband thought of her. Frigid. A cold, sexless creature.

How was she supposed to respond? Was she supposed to tell him the truth? That his "unwanted advances" had inflamed her? That she'd lain in bed fantasizing about her wedding night, about him, until she'd had to touch herself to relieve the desperate yearning?

Never could Charli bring herself to admit such things, and it wouldn't have mattered if she had. He wanted her frigid. He wanted some kind of neat, dry marriage without the complications of passion.

She thought about his decision to forgo a wedding band. "All that about your social life. You meant other women."

His gaze slid away. "As I said, I'll do nothing to cause you embarrassment. I'll be...circumspect in my activities."

He was going to see other women. Have sex with other women. Charli's stomach clenched, and for a few moments she feared she might get sick.

"What about children?" she asked when she could speak.

He looked at her. "Is that why this bothers you? Charli, I..." His expression softened. "I thought we understood each other. I assumed you realized there would be no children. I take responsibility for the mis-communication. It was, well, an awkward thing to have to discuss, and I see now that I botched it. I should've been more direct."

He sat on the edge of the bed, but didn't touch her. She stared at her knees.

"I'm sorry for the mix-up," he said. "Did you have your heart set on having children?"

How could she tell him that she'd never had her heart set on having children because she'd never thought she'd get married? She'd never dared to assume she'd become a mother, but she'd hoped, dreamed, and during this past euphoric week she'd even chosen names: Michelle, Peter, Gabriella, Christian, perhaps even a Grant Junior.

She didn't look at him. She knew if she did, she'd have no hope of holding back the tears.

The mattress dipped slightly and she sensed him moving, perhaps reaching for her. If so, he drew back without touching her.

"It'll work." His voice was gruff. "You'll see. Two people can be a family, Charli. You've got your teaching career, and you'll be kept busy running this house, entertaining—just like you did for your folks. Of course, managing a household like this will be different from what you're accustomed to, but no less challenging. When would you even have time for kids?"

His words were meant to console her, she knew. Who needed kids when there was a household to run? Who needed a loving physical relationship with her husband when there were parties to plan?

Just like you did for your folks.

"I don't mean to imply you'll be doing all the work yourself, of course," Grant hastily added. "I have people come in to clean, and you can hire anyone else you want. You'll have help when we entertain, too—after all, I'll want my wife by my side chatting up the senior partners, not sweating away in the kitchen."

Charli raised her face to his at last. "Why?"

"I told you—"

"You told me why you want our marriage to be platonic. But why get married at all? You have the kind of life that suits you—you're set in your ways. You said so yourself."

"I told you you're the right woman for me, and I meant that."

"The right woman how?" He didn't love her, and

she now knew that wouldn't change. Love was part of that whole messy emotional roller coaster her husband wanted no part of. "You said that everything that's important, you already know about me. What do you know about me that made you want to marry me?"

"Well, partly it's your temperament." He seemed to choose his words with care. "You're good-natured, Charli. Modest. Accommodating. Undemanding."

She heard the part left unsaid. *Submissive. Obedient.*

"And you know how much I admire your domestic and organizational skills," he added.

Last week when Grant had told her she was the right woman for him, she'd been so pathetically naive she'd thought he meant he wanted to wake up next to her, raise babies with her, share himself with her in every way.

For thirty years she'd known she wasn't the type of woman men thought of that way. What had made her think anything had changed?

"Still," she said, "you've been a bachelor all these years. Why get married now?" She could practically hear his canny lawyer's brain working overtime. "Be honest, Grant. I have a right to know."

His expression softened in resignation, and in that instant she knew she didn't want to hear whatever he was about to say.

"It was…the right time. Charli, I—"

"The right time how?" She lifted her chin. "It's all right. I just want to know."

His jaw tightened. "Careerwise," he said quietly.

"It's the right time in terms of my career. I told you I'm trying to make partner."

"And it helps to have a wife?"

"It's a requirement. At least in my firm. When Frank Van Cleave brought me on board, it was with the assumption that I'd make partner fairly quickly. That was five years ago—it wasn't supposed to take this long. But the firm is ultraconservative and—well, the bottom line is, an unmarried associate doesn't have a prayer of making that leap."

"And that's important to you," she said. "Becoming a partner."

"It's everything."

"Why?"

He said nothing for a moment, and Charli sensed he regretted his spontaneous answer, regretted revealing even that much about himself.

"It's late." He stood. "I think we've hashed out enough for one night."

Charli knew when she was being dismissed. Modest, undemanding women like her always did. She slid off the bed, bade her husband good-night and went to her room.

7

"GOTTA HAND IT TO YOU," Sam said. "Once you make up your mind about something, you don't let grass grow under your feet."

Grant stood with Sam on the Kauffmans' spacious back deck, sipping his usual: Maker's Mark bourbon with a splash of water. It was unseasonably warm for early May, the late afternoon sky an unbroken azure. He followed Sam's gaze to Charli, his bride of one week, chatting with Linda by the elaborate wooden play set located halfway down the Kauffmans' half-acre backyard. Sam and Linda's two young sons cavorted on the swings and slide while their infant daughter dozed nearby in her net-sided playpen.

Grant viewed this visit as his wife's first "test"—of her poise, comportment and conversational skills—though he hadn't put it to her that way, of course. Nevertheless, she knew, he was sure. He saw it in the guarded glances she sent his way, in the telltale pauses before she spoke, as if she were weighing every word coming out of her mouth. As much as Grant wanted her to make a positive first impression, he wished she could relax and enjoy herself at the same time.

Perhaps someday she would, when being "on"

every time they socialized with his colleagues had become second nature for her.

He also wished she'd smile. The polite smiles she bestowed on their hosts were her first since their wedding night—at least the first he'd seen.

For the dozenth time, Grant wished he'd been a lot more blunt when he'd discussed their upcoming marriage. He'd *planned* to be blunt. He'd planned to spell it out in no uncertain terms. What he hadn't counted on was how difficult it would be to do so face-to-face. Somehow, after he'd put the ring on her finger—and she'd come around after her dead faint!—he hadn't had the stomach for an unvarnished recitation of the grim details.

He'd been *proposing*, for God's sake, and she'd been overcome with giddy excitement, and so when the moment of truth had come, he'd opted for tact, assuming—perhaps hoping—she'd comprehend the gist of his message: that theirs would be a sexless marriage.

The result of all this well-meaning tact was that his bride had been bewildered and embarrassed on their wedding night—and he'd been left shaken as hell. God knew he never meant to hurt her.

Nevertheless, he was determined to follow through with his original plan. Too much was at stake for him to start second-guessing himself now. What he'd told Charli last week was true: this marriage would work. He was a take-charge guy, accustomed to calling the shots in all aspects of his life and work. He wished things had gotten off to a smoother start, but he was confident the rough patch was behind them.

He only wished she'd smile.

"Come on," Sam said, leading the way down the deck steps and across the lawn to the women. "If we leave them alone too long, who knows what kind of insurrectionist ideas Linda will plant in your wife's mind. The honeymoon'll be over before it's begun, buddy."

"Did I hear the word *honeymoon?*" Linda addressed herself to Grant as the men joined them. "As in the honeymoon your new bride did *not* get?"

Grinning, he put up his hands as if to ward off her wrath. "Did Charli show you her consolation prize for having to wait three months for her wedding trip?"

Charli toyed with the emerald-and-diamond bangle bracelet on her wrist. "It was too extravagant. I don't mind waiting."

Linda clucked Charli to silence and gave her a sisterly pat on the back. "He's a newlywed, and still besotted. Let him give you jewelry. The well usually runs dry around the time the first major appliance goes."

"What did I tell you, Grant?" Sam said with a laugh. "My wife's a bad influence. Colin!" he called to his five-year-old son, who was roughhousing with his three-year-old brother at the top of the slide. "Cut that out. Someone's going to get hurt."

A mewling cry drew their attention to the playpen and little Alice, just awakened from her nap. Sam picked up the baby, who was wearing one of those stretchy one-piece outfits—pink with white ducks marching across the front.

"Does she need a fresh diaper?" Linda asked. When

her husband shrugged, she added, "This is your third child, Sam. I know you know how to check."

"I'm no good at that sort of thing." Sam's guileless look didn't fool anyone. "It takes a woman's special touch."

"Yeah, right. Train Grant early," Linda advised Charli, as she gave Alice's thickly padded bottom a cursory feel. "Make sure he's changed a couple of diapers before you even leave the hospital. She's dry."

"Oh." Sam glanced from Charli to Grant. "Are more congratulations in order?"

"What?" Grant said. "You mean...? No. She's not—we're not, uh, expecting." He glanced at Charli; if she was disturbed by the direction the conversation had taken, she gave no clue. Not that that stubborn pride of hers would let her. Still, finding out on her wedding night that she'd never become a mother must have been quite a blow.

"Well, we were just wondering," Sam said. "The rushed wedding and all..."

Linda rolled her eyes. "Way to go, slick."

He turned on his wife. "Well, we *were* wondering!"

While Grant mentally fumbled for a way out of this conversational sinkhole, Charli spoke up.

"You aren't the first to ask," she said, kindly. "It's only natural, under the circumstances. Do you mind if I hold her?" As she lifted Alice into her arms, she said, "Is that a tooth coming through? Didn't you say she was only four months old?"

"Four and a half months." Sam grabbed a cloth diaper from the playpen and draped Charli's shoulder. "You'll need this for the drool."

"Colin didn't get his first tooth till he was six months old," Linda interjected, "and Jesse was even later. And oh, did they carry on! Teething doesn't seem to bother Alice much, she just drools up a storm from it."

"She may be as uncomfortable as the boys were," Charli suggested, "but she just doesn't make a big fuss."

"That's my girl." Sam beamed. "One tough broad."

"Have you tried giving her a cold carrot to teeth on?"

Grant was in awe. Within about twenty seconds Charli had smoothly alleviated her hosts' embarrassment and distracted them with a topic of absorbing interest to them.

She'd just racked up a few points on his social-skills tally sheet.

There it was. The smile he'd hoped to see. He'd wanted to put it there himself, but at the moment she only had eyes for Alice. Charli addressed the baby in soft, friendly tones, employing animated facial expressions, which Alice attempted to mimic.

"You're a natural," Sam told her.

"I've had lots of practice with my nieces and nephews."

Charli's radiant smile completely transformed her, reminding Grant of how she'd been those weeks before the wedding, how their relationship had been, natural and affectionate. They'd get that back, he told himself—once she'd settled in to married life and her role as his wife, once she'd fully come to terms with the unforeseen reality of a childless union. It was just a matter of time.

Sam asked, "How's the Walston divorce coming along?"

"Oh, no shop talk!" Linda complained.

"It took some doing," Grant said, "but we found the assets Walston was hiding. A pile of cash he'd squirreled away, offshore investments, real estate he'd transferred to other people's names. All done within the year before he left his wife. The judge was not amused."

Sam smirked. "So much for pleading reversal of fortune."

"He thought he'd covered his tracks, but my investigator, Romano, knows all the tricks. If Walston had gotten away with it, his wife would've lost the house, everything."

Charli said, "A private investigator. That must've been expensive. The wife—your client—could she afford him?"

"No way," he said. "She's a full-time mother, hasn't had a job since before she married the bastard eleven years ago. And he made sure she had nothing in her name, nothing to show for her economic contribution to their marriage—raising his children, making his life comfortable, everything she did that allowed him to devote himself to his work and make all that money he claimed didn't exist."

"The husband will be made to pay for the investigation," Sam explained, "as well as her legal fees."

"Sometimes—" Grant raised his glass in a toast

"—there is justice. Kinda nice when it works out that way, huh?"

Charli was looking at him a little oddly, as if something about his career—about *him*—didn't jibe with her preconceived notions.

Alice started fussing, reaching for her mother.

"She's hungry," Linda said, as she took her. "I'd better go nurse her." She crossed the lawn and disappeared into the house.

"Still like your Infiniti?" Sam asked.

"I like it so much I'm getting another one, for Charli."

"I told you." Charli cast a nervous glance at Sam before murmuring, "I don't need another car. My Camry is only three years old."

"You're turning down a brand-new Infiniti?" Laughing, Sam slid his arm around Charli. "This girl must really love you, Grant."

Charli's response was a weak smile, obviously forced. She didn't meet Grant's eyes.

From the play set came a sharp yip of pain. They looked over to see three-year-old Jesse sprawled in the bare dirt under one of the swings, Colin backing up guiltily. Before Sam could reach them, Jesse sprang to his feet and rushed his big brother in a tangle of kicking feet and flailing fists. Sam separated the two and picked up the smaller one. Tears of outrage streaming down his flushed little face, Jesse was screaming at his brother, something about him being a big stupid dope and a doo-doo head.

Colin shrugged, all innocence. "He fell."

"He pushed too hard!"

Jesse wore red shorts and a red-and-white striped shirt. Charli gently brushed the dirt off his knees, scored with mild abrasions. "You just need to get these cleaned up."

Sam said, "Let's go inside, big guy, and I'll put some peroxide on them."

"*No!*" Jesse cried. "Roxide hurts!"

Sam gave Grant and Charli a long-suffering look. "One of us usually has to hold him down."

Charli said, "Oh, I'll bet Jesse's big enough to put the peroxide on himself."

Father and son blinked at her. Sam got that why-didn't-I-think-of-that look and said, "How about it, Jesse? Are you big enough to clean your own boo-boos?"

Jesse pondered this. "Colin doesn't clean his own boo-boos. Colin cries."

"I do not!" Colin yelled. "You're the big crybaby!"

Sam asked, "Do you want to show Colin how you can clean your own boo-boos?"

Jesse nodded vigorously. "*I'll* do it!"

"Just give me a few minutes," Sam called over his shoulder as he steered his boys toward the house.

"Take your time," Grant said. When they were alone, he turned to Charli. "What made you think of that? Letting him wield the peroxide?"

"Sometimes the worst thing is not so much the pain, but the feeling of powerlessness. If you do it yourself, it still hurts, but at least you're in control and not at someone else's mercy."

Her words brought to mind their first date, when

Charli had tried so hard to cut the evening short, once she'd realized he wanted to ditch her.

At least you're in control and not at someone else's mercy.

He placed his palm on her back and ushered her across the lawn to the teak bench swing suspended by chains from the limb of a venerable old oak tree. They sat at opposite ends of the pale wooden bench, leaving about two feet of space between them.

Grant placed his drink on the grass and settled into the corner, half facing his wife. He started lazily rocking the swing. Charli looked fresh and springlike today in a short-sleeved, mint-colored linen dress.

His first husbandly act had been to present her with a handful of credit cards to the best department stores, with instructions to have Raven and her other friends help her select some new clothes and accessories. He didn't care what she wore to work, but she needed a fashionable wardrobe for her off-hours, when he'd be presenting her to his friends and associates. As a wise man once said, you only have one chance to make a good first impression.

Charli's dress buttoned down the front and had vertical tucks sewn around the midsection, causing the material to conform more closely to her body than the droopy, unflattering sacks she usually wore. He'd caught her giving the material a discreet tug a couple of times, no doubt because she was unaccustomed to wearing anything that hinted at her womanly shape.

Light percolated through the canopy of leaves in a lacework pattern that cascaded up and down her body as the swing slowly swayed. Watching her,

Grant was reminded of the evening he'd proposed to Charli, when he'd tried to seduce her. He'd wanted her then. Holding her on his lap, kissing her, fondling her through her clothes—it hadn't been enough. Nor had he intended it to be. He'd had little doubt they'd end up in bed.

Until her lack of response had finally registered in his lust-fogged mind. She'd accepted his kisses and caresses without complaint, but with little enthusiasm, as docile and accommodating in this as in everything else.

But her docility had its limits, and he hadn't been surprised when she'd refused to sleep with him. Obviously Charli had a low sex drive—which, he'd realized in retrospect, was a good thing, considering the nature of their marriage.

Grant couldn't help but wonder whether his wife's aversion to physical intimacy was due to a naturally low libido or disagreeable experiences in her past. At age thirty, even a wallflower like Charli had to have some sort of past, sexually speaking. Perhaps the fellow who'd taken her virginity had been clumsy or selfish. If her first encounters had left her unsatisfied, that might explain her dislike for sex.

Which is a good thing, he reminded himself, yet again.

Speculating on his bride's past soured Grant's mood, although he didn't imagine there'd been too many men. His annoyance was based on instinct, he reasoned, a typical male territorial response. She was his wife, after all. He had bound her to him by law if nothing else.

Of course, if *he'd* been her first, Grant thought with a secret smile, she'd probably have a totally different attitude about sex. He'd have initiated her patiently, lovingly. He'd have devoted himself to her pleasure, touching and tasting and tormenting every inch of her until she was sobbing with desire, until her world had shrunk to the relentless, knife-edged craving and the promise of relief only he could provide.

She'd have clawed at him and wrapped herself around him and welcomed him into her untried body with eager cries of fulfillment.

Grant felt himself stir. Damn. He shifted on the bench swing, forcing his thoughts away from the graphic image of his shy, staid wife flushed and panting, lifting herself to him as he plunged into her slick heat.

Against his will, he'd found himself thinking about her that way, looking at her that way, too often during the past week. It wasn't that he found her desirable— he'd known from the start she wasn't his type. His X-rated thoughts were obviously a perverse response to the fact that she was sexually indifferent to him and, by his own choice, off-limits. If she were eager and available, he'd probably be able to go an hour or two without wondering how she looked naked and sweating.

If only he hadn't seen her in that semisheer negligee on their wedding night. The low-cut bodice had cupped her full, round breasts like a lover's hands. Her dusky nipples had been clearly visible, thrusting against the lacy fabric. Her color had been high, and there'd been something besides her usual shyness in the smile she'd given him as he'd entered his bedroom, something that could almost be called excitement.

At the time he'd been too stunned and dismayed to assess all these telling details. But since then, he'd occasionally caught her casting lingering glances his way, causing him to speculate that perhaps his prudish little bride wasn't as prudish as he'd assumed.

And why did that prospect excite him, when it would only wreak havoc with his carefully laid plans?

She wasn't giving him any damn lingering looks! They were a product of his sex-starved imagination, nothing more. He had to get laid, and soon. After all, *he* wasn't the one with the diminished sex drive. He'd continue to see other women, but discreetly; he had no desire to embarrass Charli, or jeopardize his standing with the firm, by engaging in a public affair.

Charli crossed her legs, drawing Grant's gaze to the small patch of thigh that slid within view. The hem of her dress fell to within a few inches of her ankles, but the lowest button was just above her knees. Her movement caused the bottom of the dress to part. She yanked on the material to cover herself.

Grant leaned over and flicked it open again. "This dress is made to show some leg, Charli."

She stared at him a moment, then uncrossed her legs and pulled the sides of the dress closed. Grant detected a morsel of defiance as she said, "I thought modesty was one of my virtues."

He recalled saying something like that on their wedding night. "Well, being so damn uptight isn't."

She didn't look at him. So much for putting a smile on her face.

He stopped rocking the swing. "I didn't mean to snap. I'm just trying to help you...adjust."

After a thick silence she said, "I seem to need a lot of adjustment."

"What do you mean? Because I wanted you to have a nice new wardrobe? Most wives would kill for—"

"It's not like you were *asking*." She clamped her mouth shut, obviously regretting her impulsive words.

"Charli." Grant tried to look her in the eye, but she stared into the distance, hands planted in her lap. Quietly he said, "Don't ever be afraid to tell me what's on your mind." No response. "Charli. Look at me."

She didn't. Grant edged closer and put his arm around her shoulders. He felt her tense.

"Our marriage is a partnership of equals," he said, lightly stroking her upper arm with his fingertips. "I want to know what's bothering you. If I've somehow stepped over the line, tell me."

She started to speak, but seemed unable to find the words. Finally she sighed in frustration. "I know I need to learn things. I guess I just didn't realize how much."

"Is it a little overwhelming? Going a little too fast for you?"

Charli raised her face to his. She looked so vulnerable, something clutched inside his chest. "I guess so," she said in a small voice. "I can't seem to do anything right."

"That's not true. Some things are just new to you, that's all. Like supervising Anna and Doreen."

"I'm not used to having other people clean my home."

"I know that. That's why I showed you how to instruct them, so things get done the way you want."

The way you *want, you mean.* He saw it in her eyes, but she didn't say it.

"I told you before," he said. "I'm set in my ways. I make no apologies for that."

"But if I decide I want things done a little differently around the house, like if I want to move some furniture or, I don't know, put up a picture or something, is that all right with you?"

Grant forced himself to say, "Of course." After a moment he added, "Just check with me first, okay?"

She nodded, and something told him she wouldn't be suggesting any changes.

He said, "It probably seems like I've been offering a lot of advice, in a lot of different areas, and I get the feeling it's not all welcome, but like I said, I'm just trying to make the adjustment easier for you."

"Maybe with some things, though, we can leave well enough alone."

"Like what?"

"Like my car. It's in mint condition. And I like it, Grant. It drives well and it's comfortable and I even love the color. It's the best car I've ever owned."

"But you can have a *better* car! A luxury car! Sam must've thought you were nuts, turning down a brand-new Infiniti!"

"I'm sorry if I embarrassed you in front of your friend."

"You didn't, Charli. That's not what this is about."

"Is it the image? You don't want people—important people—seeing your wife driving a three-year-old midpriced sedan?"

What was he supposed to say when she put it like that? "Fine," he said. "Do what you want. I won't pretend to understand your reasoning, but it's up to you what you drive."

He watched that simple truth register in her mind. "I'll stick with my Camry, then."

"Fine."

A ponderous silence descended, interrupted only by the sounds of a bird warbling overhead and a lawn mower somewhere in the distance. Charli twisted the emerald bangle bracelet on her wrist. Finally she said, "Grant, do you think I married you for your money?"

"What brought that on?"

"Do you?"

He sighed. Why did they have to talk about this? Why did she have to make it sound so crass? "Charli, there's nothing wrong with you wanting to better your situation. Do you imagine I think less of you because of that?"

"I wasn't destitute before I married you," she said stiffly. "My family isn't poor. They're hardworking, middle-class people."

"I never said they—" He broke off with a curse. "Of course you weren't destitute. But don't try to tell me you never had to pinch pennies, or make sacrifices. You're ashamed to admit my income and my standard of living influenced your decision to marry me, but you shouldn't be. You said it yourself—we're not a couple of twenty-year-olds with stars in our eyes. We're both mature, realistic people."

Her voice was strained. "You can't think of any other reason I'd have married you?"

Grant's arm was still around her shoulders, but now his fingers tightened into a fist. Every muscle in his body tensed. He stared at a squirrel scampering along the top of the wooden fence and said, "I think we're compatible, certainly. Otherwise I wouldn't have proposed this arrangement."

It wasn't what she wanted to hear, he knew. *Don't do this,* he silently pleaded. *Don't try to make this marriage into something it's not. That can only lead to disaster.*

He felt her turn, sensed her gaze on his profile. He expected her to pursue the issue, but instead she asked, "Did you grow up with the same comfortable lifestyle you have now?"

Frowning, he faced her. "Where did that come from?"

She shrugged, but her eyes never left his. They looked liquid and bottomless in the stippled light, the color of dark, rich coffee, with streaks of amaretto near the pupils. "You said you grew up in Pennsylvania, in a small town. I was just wondering—"

"I don't talk about that part of my life."

She hesitated, searching his eyes. "You said you're estranged from your folks."

"I told you, Charli, it's not up for discussion."

She blinked at his harsh tone, and drew back.

He practically growled in frustration. "Look, it's not

like I'm keeping any deep, dark secrets from you. There's nothing interesting or exciting in how I grew up, nothing worth talking about."

She appeared ready to argue with him. Thankfully, she seemed to think better of it, and held her tongue.

From the deck Linda called, "If I can tear you two lovebirds away from that swing, the chicken marsala's getting cold."

Breathing a silent sigh of relief, Grant rose and offered Charli his hand.

8

"LET THE NEWLYWEDS sit next to each other!" Mama screeched.

Charli's brother Eddie quickly vacated his chair, and Charli let herself be jostled into it. Another of her brothers, Paul, standing on the fringes of the crowd near the makeshift bar—where else?—called out, "No way. Who knows what those two'll get up to under the table? There are minors present!"

This was met with rude guffaws from the twenty or so adults present, and most of the youngsters, as well. Charli studiously avoided looking at her husband, seated next to her at her nephew John's dining table in the home he shared with his wife and twin daughters in Sunnyside, Queens. The room was crammed with people pressing in on them from all sides and spilling into the kitchen and living room.

The twins turned one year old today, and the extended family had gathered this Wednesday evening after work to watch them blow out the candle on their birthday cake. John and his wife, Moira Sullivan-Rossi, had named their daughters Swanhilda and Valkyrie, from Norse mythology, despite the fact that there wasn't a drop of Norse blood on either side of the family tree.

The babies were fraternal rather than identical, as

different in looks and temperament as any two siblings could be. Val was already a willful little handful, with green eyes and red hair like her mother. Mellow-tempered Swan, with her dark curls and thick-lashed, amber eyes, outweighed her petite sister by a good five pounds.

The babies sat at one end of the table, side by side in matching high chairs. No sooner had they extinguished the candle—with a little help from their cousins—than Val thrust her tiny hands into the frosting, smearing the writing and the pink and yellow icing flowers. Swan calmly planted her two sucking fingers in her mouth, taking in the ensuing mayhem with her usual thoughtful regard. Val wasn't giving up the candle without a fight.

Grant leaned closer to Charli. She felt his palm on her back, his warm breath on the side of her face. Amid the uproar he whispered into her ear, "I'll give the redhead a scholarship to law school. We could use her at the firm."

"Hey, Grant, no talking dirty in front of Nonni!" Donna's husband, Artie, hollered. Grandma Rossi, in her place of honor at the other end of the table, shot back something in Italian that had the older relatives hooting with glee.

"They've been married a week and a half," Charli's other sister, Angie, announced. "They're allowed to neck in public."

"Good thing we got them outta their house," Robby said. "I hear the sheets were about to catch fire."

"Shut your mouth!" Mama whacked her youngest son on the back of the head, which only made him laugh harder. "You don't talk like that at your nieces' birthday."

Papa said, "The boy's just having a little fun, Betty. Leave him alone."

"Just having a little fun!" Mama hollered. "He can have a little fun without the gutter talk!"

Grant risked another intimate murmur. "Looks like we've created quite a stir."

Charli's face burned. "I'm sorry. I should've warned you. They were like this when all my brothers and sisters got married."

"Ah, a family tradition. How utterly heartwarming. Honestly, Charli, I can't believe you're apologizing." He rubbed her back in a circle. "They're just having a little fun."

Charli faced him then, and caught her breath. His teasing grin transformed him completely, making him look as mischievous and carefree as a schoolboy. She had a glimpse of what he must have looked like as a youth.

Had he been mischievous and carefree? Somehow Charli knew the answer to that question, without asking.

Because the questions she *had* asked had gone unanswered. She'd never known anyone as secretive about his past. Briefly it had occurred to her that her husband might be hiding something really awful, like a criminal record. But if he'd been convicted of a crime, wouldn't he have had trouble becoming a lawyer? Certainly a stuffy firm like Farman, Van Cleave and Holm wouldn't have touched him.

No, it was something else, something so personally

devastating that he felt the need to hide it even from his wife.

Not that she thought of herself as a wife. Glorified housekeeper was more like it. As far as Charli was concerned, she'd simply exchanged one caretaking job for another. She was expected to see to her husband's comfort, keep his home the way he liked it, and above all, avoid injecting her own preferences or, God forbid, her sense of style. In a hundred little ways, Grant made it clear that her opinions on matters of taste were not to be trusted. He wasn't mean about it, he always couched it in the most diplomatic of terms, but there was no escaping the message: leave all such decisions to him.

He'd given her an almost limitless housekeeping and personal allowance—all out of his own funds. Charli had assumed they'd pool their paychecks and have joint bank accounts like other couples. He'd quickly squelched that idea, assuring her that his income was more than adequate for all their expenses, and insisting she keep her money separate in her own name, to be spent on little extras for herself, or to simply accumulate. In Grant's eyes, her financial contribution didn't even rise to the level of "second income." It was entirely superfluous.

Charli wasn't accustomed to having her hard-earned paycheck, and by extension her career, trivialized by anyone, much less the one person she was supposed to be closer to than anyone in the world. She'd quickly come to realize that the spouse who wielded the checkbook also wielded the power. Not that Grant was a tyrant, but there was never a question of who was in charge, who made all the important decisions.

Mama and Moira attempted to mop up the frosting Val had smeared on herself and her high chair, but the baby was having none of it. She emitted earsplitting shrieks and arched her back as they struggled to pull her out of her chair.

First Jesse and Colin's squabble at the Kauffmans', and now this. If Grant had been at all inclined to change his mind about having kids, Charli thought, the recent displays he'd witnessed would certainly change it right back.

She berated herself for even entertaining this particular train of thought. Grant was a thirty-nine-year-old bachelor—in spirit if not in fact—with an entrenched lifestyle and an aversion to emotional entanglements. He'd never change his mind about having children, or about having the kind of relationship with his wife that would even make them possible. To him, marriage was a cold-blooded career move. No, not *marriage*, she silently corrected herself. It was an *arrangement*. A *partnership*. Wasn't that how he always referred to it?

While everyone partook of birthday cake and ice cream, the twins opened their presents—again with a little help from their older cousins. Afterward Charli and Grant migrated to the enclosed sunporch in back of the house, where a handful of her young nieces were playing with their Barbie dolls. Grant chased a pair of calico house cats off the bamboo love seat upholstered in a loud jungle print, and sat with Charli.

"We can leave anytime," she said quietly. "Don't feel like you have to spend all evening here."

"No problem. We'll stay a little longer—don't want to wolf down the cake and run."

Charli had the distinct impression Grant actually enjoyed hanging out with her family, as bizarre as that seemed. Not exactly the behavior of an entrenched bachelor. Perhaps he was pretending, for her sake.

Little Val charged into the room in a kind of toddling run, looking like a mechanical clown doll with her wispy orange hair and vivid color-block coveralls. She stopped short at the sight of Charli and Grant, upsetting her precarious balance and causing her to plop onto her thickly diapered butt.

"Val!" Moira rushed in after her, looking harried and exhausted. Swan snuggled against her mother's hip, sucking her fingers, her eyelids drooping.

Val bellowed angrily and swatted at Moira as she tried to scoop her up with her other arm. "Come on, peanut, it's bedtime." Moira turned her weary gaze on Charli and Grant. "Val started walking at ten and a half months." She sighed. "God help me."

Grant said, "Why don't you leave her with us for a bit?" Leaning over, he lifted the baby and perched her on his knee. "Something tells me this young lady's just hitting her stride."

Moira said, "Are you sure? She can be a handful."

"Oh, I think I can handle one little—" He broke off with a yelp as Val yanked a fistful of chest hair peeking over the open collar of his dove-gray polo shirt. Gently he disentangled her tiny fingers while she cackled like her great-great-grandma Rossi.

"Didn't you hear him?" Charli cast her nephew's wife an amused glance. "He can handle one little baby."

Moira smirked. "All right. Give her to John when you feel like flinging her out the window. I'm going to put Swan in her crib and make myself a drink."

Val didn't seem inclined to relinquish Grant's chest hair, so he buttoned up, thwarting her. "You're just a little devil, aren't you?" he asked the baby, his hazel eyes sparking with humor. "You've got the world all figured out, don't you?"

"*Ba-ba-ba-ba-ba-ba-ba!*" Val crowed, tugging furiously on his shirt buttons.

"Definitely a litigator," he told Charli. "She's got an objection to everything."

Charli tried to absorb the remarkable spectacle of Grant Sterling dandling an infant on his knee, cuddling her, *entertaining* the little hellion!

Of course, this baby he could simply give back to her parents when she got to be a nuisance, without risk of those dreaded emotional entanglements he so abhorred. Still, Charli wouldn't have thought he had it in him.

"I really do appreciate your making time for this," she said. "Family get-togethers like this...well, it's just something that has to be done."

"I told you, I don't mind." Grant amused the baby with one of the Barbie dolls close at hand, this one wearing only a striped bikini top and a hank of matted platinum hair. Val gave it a good slobbery inspection. "I'll have to stay extra late at the office tomorrow, though, to make up for it."

"Oh. Well, sure." Grant worked late most evenings—at least, that was what he told Charli. She felt like the typical jealous wife, wondering if her husband was indeed working late on a case, or was instead engaging in a little extramarital sport. Of course, she had no right to feel jealous—according to the terms of their *arrangement*.

She knew that when he did see other women, he'd keep it to himself, not out of shame or secrecy but to avoid those awkward conversations he hated, and also because it was simply none of her business.

Her husband's sexual liaisons were none of her business.

Charli felt that sick twisting of her gut again, just as she did every time she thought about Grant kissing someone else, caressing someone else, making love with someone else.

Last Saturday he'd tossed his golf bag into the trunk of his car and disappeared for the entire day and part of the evening. "I won't be home for dinner," he'd told her, but by then she was already accustomed to dining alone in that big, empty house.

Had he really been playing golf? With whom? What had he done the rest of the day? Where had he eaten dinner?

And again, with whom?

Charli agonized over these questions, a fruitless exercise in self-torture. This was what married life would be for her, and she couldn't even share her misery with anyone. She didn't dare tell Raven or Amanda or Sunny about it—she was too ashamed. Her friends thought she'd found the happiness she'd always craved. She was their second Wedding Ring success story, and they were deliriously happy for her. She just couldn't face them with the humiliating truth.

And what good would it do anyway? They'd only tell her what she already knew: married or not, she was bound by the Wedding Ring pact and the three-month rule. She had to stick it out for that long at least.

The fact was, Charli knew she'd stick it out for the duration, till death did them part. Her pride wouldn't allow her to go crawling back to her parents' home and her old life. How could she admit to her family, her friends, the entire world, that plain, unlovable Charli Rossi Sterling couldn't even get her husband to share her bed?

No one watching Grant now, seated next to his wife and engaged in a lively game of peekaboo with her little grandniece, would see anything out of the ordinary.

Charli came to her feet. If she sat there any longer wondering who her husband was planning to "work late" with tomorrow night, she'd break down right here in front of the baby and Grant and her nieces and all those simpering, bosomy Barbies. "I'm going to see if they can use any help cleaning up," she mumbled, and slipped out of the room.

It had to be her imagination, but she thought he looked a little disappointed to see her go.

She passed through the dining room, where the men had congregated to talk baseball—"First place now, but wait till the all-star break!"—into the living room, where the women were vying for most unsavory childbirth story: "Nine pounds ten ounces, my God, that kid tore me from stem to stern!"

Charli doubled back along the stair-side hallway to the kitchen, where she found Grandma Rossi sitting alone at the dinette table, drying flatware.

"Nonni, you don't have to do that. All this'll air-dry in the dish drain."

"Spots." Nonni vigorously wiped a fork with a kitchen towel.

"Let Moira worry about spots."

"Eh, that girl, she gets no rest with those twins. That little redhead— *Dio mio!* Moira should use paper and plastic. Throw it away. *Fffttt!* No work."

Charli grabbed another towel and dropped into the chair across from her grandmother. She pulled a pile of wet spoons closer and started to work on them. "We can't stay too much longer. But I'm glad we got a chance to wish the girls a happy birthday."

Nonni gave her a significant look. "You take that man of yours home, Carlotta. That's where you two belong, married not even two weeks."

"Nonni..." Charli rolled her eyes as she dried a spoon. "Not you, too."

"I see the way he looks at you, your Grant—*con passione.*" Her eyes got misty. "It's the same way my Sergio used to look at me."

I sincerely doubt that, Charli thought. She recalled how her grandpa used to look at her grandma, the adoration he never tried to conceal, spiked with just a hint of deviltry, even after six decades of marriage.

"That look, it gives you *molto bambini.*" Grinning

wickedly, Nonni waggled a fork at Charli. "I hope you got a lotta bedrooms in that big house of yours."

"You're wrong, Nonni. Not every husband feels that way about his wife. Grant...he doesn't look at me with...*passione*." After a few moments she dropped her eyes to the spoon in her hand, unable to hold Nonni's insightful gaze.

"You don't see it, the way your man looks at you." Nonni leaned toward Charli, speaking quietly. "Not all the time. Only when he thinks no one sees. That one, he thinks he's clever. *Molto intelligente*. Luisa Rossi—" she pointed to her own eye "—she sees."

"Oh, Nonni...if Grant is giving me any special looks, it's because he's too polite to tell me he wants to go home. And not so we can—" She broke off with a ragged sigh.

What would Charli's beloved grandmother and lifelong confidante say if she knew that Charli was still a virgin, that she would die a virgin, that there would be no *bambini* to fill the bedrooms of that big house on the Sound?

Nonni sat back in her chair, nodding sagely. "There are ways."

"Ways? What do you mean?"

"A clever woman, she knows how to bring out the *passione* in her man."

Unless her man is saving his passione *for other women*. Charli reached for another spoon. Her chin began to quiver. She didn't dare look into her grandmother's wise brown eyes.

Nonni continued, "You just gotta use your..." She

muttered in Italian, searching for the word. "Feminine wiles!" she blurted triumphantly.

Charli gave in to a watery chuckle, treading a fine line now between hilarity and tears. Since when did plain, unlovable Charli Rossi Sterling possess feminine wiles? "Maybe I should just wave my magic wand. That would have a better chance of working."

"There are ways to keep a man's interest," Nonni said, with that astute expression Charli knew so well. "Like the look you give him. Or the look you *don't* give him. You ignore him. You tease him. It's the way you move, the things you wear, the things you say, the way you say them.... Pretty soon you're all he can think about, an *ossessione.*"

An obsession. Charli tried to imagine her husband obsessing about her, desiring her, watching her the way Nonni claimed he did.

It could never happen.

Could it?

Suddenly Charli was angry with herself for even entertaining the possibility, angry at her grandmother for planting the idea in her mind.

Nonni was watching her closely. She raised one iron-gray eyebrow, nodding with authority. "Feminine wiles."

"I don't have any feminine wiles, Nonni."

"*Assurdità!* You got lots of 'em, they're just a little rusty."

"Use 'em or lose 'em," Charli muttered.

"*Sì!* That's right! You ask those friends of yours for help. That Amanda. She'll tell you what to do."

"You and Amanda never agree about anything," Charli reminded her.

Nonni waved her hand dismissively. "That one, *è con esperienza.* She knows men."

"She ought to by now, she's been married and divorced twice."

Nonni muttered her disapproval.

"You ladies aren't gossiping in here, are you?" Grant asked from the doorway. From where Charli sat, he looked big and imposing and heartbreakingly handsome, wearing that tender little smile that always made something deep within her turn to slush.

The smile was nice, and always welcome, but it wasn't the kind of heated look Nonni had been talking about.

Look who I'm going to for advice on my love life, Charli thought. *A ninety-three-year-old Italian widow who married the man her parents told her to and never went on a date in her life.*

Charli rose. "Ready to go?" She noticed he'd divested himself of the redheaded terror.

"If you are." Grant leaned down and hugged Charli's grandmother. He kissed her lined cheek. "Nonni, we'll come visit you on the weekend. I'll bring you some of that special coffee you like."

There was a shop in Little Italy that sold imported espresso beans that sent the old woman into raptures.

"No, no, that *caffè, è troppo costoso,*" Nonni protested, even as her faded brown eyes lit up at the thought. "Those thieves, the prices they charge—the beans should be made of gold!"

"Okay," Grant said, "I won't get any."

"Buy me five pounds," she said. "It stays good in the freezer."

He laughed. "I'll pick it up at lunchtime tomorrow."

Then it was Charli's turn to bend over and give her grandmother a warm hug. A prickle of awareness skated down her spine. She glanced behind her in time to see Grant's gaze dart away from her bottom. He quickly recovered his stolid expression, but for an instant there'd been something else going on behind those cool hazel eyes. Something that had nothing to do with "arrangements" or "partnerships" or anything platonic.

Yesterday she wouldn't have given a second thought to that kind of casual look. Indeed, yesterday she *hadn't* given it a second thought. Browsing her memory banks, she realized this wasn't the first time she'd intercepted such a look. She'd known then that it hadn't meant anything. And now...

Now she didn't know what was real and what was wishful thinking.

They said their goodbyes to the others and headed home. The nighttime drive from Queens to their exclusive neighborhood on the North Shore of the Island took just under an hour, during which time they listened to music and didn't talk much.

Charli found herself sneaking glances at Grant in the dim interior of the car, thinking about what her grandmother had said, thinking about how some women, like Amanda, seemed to have been born with a fully functional set of feminine wiles. Was Charli missing the requisite gene, or was she simply "rusty," as Nonni had suggested?

"What was that for?" Grant asked.

"What?"

"That sigh. It sounded…weighty." The glance he cast her was part amused, part concerned. "You want to talk about it?"

She shook her head. "It's nothing. I'm just a little tired."

"We'll be home soon."

Grant did care for her, Charli knew, in his way. She didn't doubt that his offer to talk about what was on her mind was sincere—as long as the topic wasn't *too* weighty. As long as it didn't provoke any of those strong feelings, those destructive passions, he was forever on guard against.

She thought about how she'd always lived her life, as the quiet and dutiful daughter, now the quiet and dutiful wife. She thought about the one recent occasion when she'd actually asserted herself: when she'd gathered her siblings together and forced them to live up to their responsibilities regarding their parents and grandmother.

For once, she'd put her own needs and desires first. And in the process she'd learned something that had eluded her for the first thirty years of her life:

Her needs counted. Her desires counted. She deserved happiness.

She thought about the surreptitious look Grant had given in John and Moira's kitchen. And the other looks, the ones she'd dismissed because he couldn't possibly be looking at her *that* way. Thinking about her *that* way.

Maybe Nonni had learned a thing or two in her ninety-three years.

And maybe Charli deserved a husband in her bed.

9

GRANT PULLED his gray polo shirt over his head and tossed it onto his bed. They'd returned from the twins' birthday party a couple of hours earlier, and he and Charli had played a little pool in his basement game room, as they often did in the evenings. She was surprisingly good at the game—a result of having tagged along as a child when her brothers visited the local pool hall. After she'd said good-night and gone up to bed, he'd continued to knock the balls around the green felt, but without someone else to play against and banter with, his interest had quickly faded.

He used to spend hours in his game room, solo, just kicking back, Grant thought sourly. He never used to need company.

He opened the fly of his green khaki slacks and paused, listening. Music. Was Charli playing the radio?

Then he remembered she didn't have a radio in her room. Zipping up his pants, he opened his door and heard the unmistakable sound of a flute. She'd told him she played several instruments passably, in her role as a high school music teacher and band conductor, but that the flute was her favorite.

He padded barefoot to her door, which was cracked open a couple of inches. She played more than passably, he thought, surprised by the unusual syncopation and spirited tempo of the piece. This music was avant-garde, full of energy and feeling, with a Celtic flavor.

He'd have expected his wife to favor sedate, conventional songs. This was closer to the style of Ian Anderson, who played flute for the rock group Jethro Tull.

Grant edged closer and peeked into her room, dimly lit by a solitary bedside reading lamp. Charli stood at her window, staring out at the dark expanse of Long Island Sound. She wore summer pajamas made of some kind of thin T-shirt material in a pastel floral pattern—a sleeveless top over short shorts that barely covered what they were meant to. Especially now, with her body moving to the rhythm of the music, her hair swaying in a glossy dark curtain halfway down her back.

The sight of her soft, round bottom so temptingly displayed reminded him of earlier in the evening, in John and Moira's kitchen, when she'd almost caught him ogling her. These skimpy pj's left little to his imagination—an imagination that hadn't done her justice, he now saw.

Silently Grant pushed the door wider. She didn't know he was there. He knew he should make his presence known, or better yet, return to his own room. Instead he stood rooted to the spot, savoring the voyeuristic thrill of spying on his own wife in a private moment. It was a foolhardy thing to do. God knew he'd had enough trouble sleeping lately without adding this tantalizing image to the fantasies that tormented him. Yet he was helpless to move.

The music wound down at last, ending on a trilling note that pulled at something deep within him. Slowly Charli lowered the flute, still staring into the darkness beyond her window.

Grant didn't know he was going to speak until he heard his own voice. "Charli."

She started, and turned to look at him, those beautiful eyes wide and fathomless in the half-light.

He took a step into the room. "I never heard you play before. You're very good."

"Thank you." She looked at the flute in her hands. "It relaxes me, playing."

Why had he never heard his wife play her flute? Grant wondered. Why had he never asked her to play for him? He should have asked. He'd had no idea she had this in her—not just the talent, but the heart, the spirit.

The passion.

The very thing he'd made clear he didn't want from her.

Grant crossed the room and took the flute from her. The gleaming metal retained the warmth of her hands. His fingers closed around it as his gaze moved up her body, lingering on her full breasts, obviously bare under the clingy pajama top. His nostrils flared as he inhaled her warm, soapy scent.

He looked her in the eye, expecting to see discomfort at his frank scrutiny, expecting—hoping—she'd mutter an embarrassed good-night and show him the door. Instead she stared back unblinkingly. Her breasts rose and fell faster under the thin material. Was she afraid of him? Or was it something else?

Better that she feared him, he acknowledged bitterly. The *something else* could lead to nothing but grief. He had to stay focused on his goal, or the sweat and sacrifices of the last twenty-three years—not to mention the hell of his first sixteen—would have been for nothing.

Grant broke eye contact first. "Hold next Wednesday open. We're going to the ballet with the Van Cleaves."

"Next Wednesday? A week from today?"

He nodded.

"I can't make it."

"What do you mean? Of course you can make it. I have tickets to the New York City Ballet."

"I'm sorry, Grant, I have a symphonic band rehearsal that night."

"Oh, is that all? Reschedule it." He set the flute on the dresser top and turned to leave.

His wife's quiet "No" halted him in midstep. He faced her. Her chin inched up, just slightly.

"Look, Charli, this isn't some kind of whim. It's politics. It's the *Van Cleaves*. Eileen Van Cleave is mad for the ballet." Charli knew how important Frank Van Cleave was to Grant's career. "Wear that new gray-and-ivory outfit. With the sapphire necklace I gave you."

"The spring concert is next Thursday," she said. "I can't change the rehearsal dates—they were set months ago. And not just for my group. We're doing a piece with the concert choir. Everyone will be there that night. I wish you'd consulted me before you bought the tickets."

"I don't see the problem." He tossed his hands up. "Get a substitute teacher!"

His words straightened Charli's spine. For the first time, he saw genuine anger in her eyes, directed at him. As he tried to figure out why, she said, "I don't know what makes you think anyone else can sub for me, Grant. Especially for the last rehearsal before an important concert."

"What, this is about your ego?" He hadn't thought she had one.

"My *ego*?" She shook her head incredulously. "You have no idea what I do for a living, do you?"

"Look, I'm not belittling—"

"These kids are some of the finest young musicians on the Island. Symphonic band isn't some after-school activity, it's an honors course. As in five classes a week, plus private lessons and daily practice. They play the most advanced professional arrangements. Two of our seniors have gotten into Julliard, and one's going to Curtis next year. What am I supposed to do, get some...some—" she gestured angrily "—run-of-the-mill sub to come in and take my place because Frank Van Cleave's wife is crazy about the *ballet?*"

Charli was quivering with indignation. Grant was so astounded by this unprecedented display of backbone, he was momentarily speechless. What had happened to his shy bride with the tractable nature?

Charli said, "If my kids can make that kind of commitment, for four solid years, the least I can do is show up for the last rehearsal before a major concert."

Grant rubbed a hand over his jaw. "What can I say? You're right. I should've asked if you were free

Wednesday." It wasn't what she'd expected to hear, he could tell. "I'll see if I can exchange the tickets. Is the Wednesday after good for you?"

She nodded.

"Otherwise," he said, "I'll go without you. I don't want to do that, though. I want to introduce you to Frank. He's anxious to meet you."

And Grant was anxious to establish himself as a stable married man, prime partner material. He kept that part to himself, but something in his wife's watchful expression told him she'd read between the lines.

"Listen," he said, "this concert of yours. It's next Thursday?"

"That's right."

"Because I'd like to be there."

"You don't have to do that."

Grant almost smiled. Before Charli, he'd never considered stubborn pride to be an appealing trait. "I want to," he said, surprised to discover it was true.

Her gaze dropped to the cream carpet under her bare feet. "You usually have to work late."

"Well, I'll make an exception."

Charli looked up then, studying him. Finally she said, "I wouldn't want to hamper your social life."

"What does my social life have to do with my work-load?" As he watched her struggle for a response, the truth struck Grant. "You think I'm lying to you? That when I say I'm working late, I'm seeing other women?"

"Well, I...I didn't...I mean, I thought..."

"I'm not going to lie to you, Charli. What made you think I would?"

She took a deep breath. "I figured, since you hadn't mentioned any, um, dates…"

"What do you expect me to do, report to you every time I—" He broke off with an exasperated sigh. Why did they have to talk about this?

Just when he expected a blushing retreat, she looked him square in the eye and said, "I'm not asking you to report to me, Grant. I just don't want you to feel you have to cover up your…activities."

He gave her a wry smile. "The errant husband, slipping around on the side, concocting excuses for his whereabouts? That's the kind of duplicitous nonsense I'd hoped to avoid when I proposed our arrangement."

"So does that mean you haven't seen anyone else since the wedding? I mean, since you're so busy at the firm—"

"My outside activities are not subject to discussion," he said imperiously, hoping to stifle this topic for good. "I told you, I'll be discreet. That's all you need to know."

She returned his level stare for long, strained moments. At last she shrugged and said, "It's probably best that way." Grant started to breathe a sigh of relief until she added, "I have no desire to report every little thing to you, either."

Charli lifted her flute and tucked it into the velvet-lined instrument case lying open on her bed. She closed and latched the case and carried it to her closet, where she slid it onto one of the high shelves.

Grant watched this process in silence, as his fingers

clenched and his pulse whooshed in his ears. Finally he said, "What do you mean?"

His words brought her head around, as if she'd forgotten he was there. Another shrug. "Just that I agree with what you said."

"No, I mean..." She couldn't have meant what it sounded like. Not *Charli!* She crossed to her dresser and picked up her hairbrush. Grant followed close behind. "I'm just, you know, curious about exactly what you meant by that."

He met her dark gaze in the mirror over the dresser as she started to brush her hair, drawing the bristles through the lustrous strands slowly, almost sensually. Her movements caused her breasts to lift, and sway a little with each downstroke of the brush. Grant's mouth felt dry. He forced his eyes back to hers.

She said, "Don't worry, Grant. You're not the only one who knows how to be discreet."

That whooshing in his ears got louder. "Discreet about what?"

Setting down the brush, she lifted her hair off her nape, letting it fall in a shimmering curtain down her back, enveloping him in her womanly fragrance.

His voice was tight as he repeated, "Discreet about what, Charli?"

"We'll do nothing to embarrass each other. Isn't that what we discussed? Keeping our private liaisons private?"

What's this "we" stuff? his mind raged. At the time they'd discussed all this, he'd spoken only of himself, of his own actions. He'd simply assumed...

Never assume. Some virtuoso lawyer, forgetting a basic rule like that.

But this was *Charli!* Mr. and Mrs. Rossi's mousy, sexless daughter.

He thought about her suspicions concerning his late hours at the office, where he often worked until eight or nine. Classes at the school where Charli taught ended a little after two-thirty in the afternoon. Most days she stayed an hour or so to meet with students or attend faculty meetings. That still left...

A hell of a lot of time to be "discreet"!

"Grant," she said, "you're crowding me."

Unconsciously he'd pressed against her from behind. He stepped back. She glanced pointedly at her old-fashioned alarm clock. "I have to get up at six." When he made no move, she added, "You have to be up even earlier. We'd better turn in."

His voice was a low, menacing rumble. "You're not seeing anyone else."

She cocked her head, smiling at him in the mirror. "You see? I *do* know how to be discreet."

Grant grabbed her shoulders and spun her to face him. He backed her against the dresser, rattling the bottles and hair things and that dilapidated old jewelry box she refused to let him replace.

"Who?" he demanded.

"Grant, what's gotten into you?" She tried to squirm out of his grasp, but he gripped her shoulders harder.

"Answer me, damn it!" He gave her a little shake. "Who is he?"

"We talked about our *arrangement*, remember? My outside activities are none of your business."

"You're my wife!" he barked. "What you do and who you do it with sure as hell *is* my business!"

She gaped at him. "Are you telling me you expect me to adhere to a double standard? As in, you're allowed to have outside relationships, but I'm not?"

Grant shoved her away, breathing hard, wondering how much it hurt to put your fist through a mirror.

"Because if that's what you had in mind," she continued, "you should've said so at the beginning. I'd never agree to a sexist *arrangement* like that."

He groped for a way to rebut her words without coming off as the chauvinist troglodyte he was beginning to feel like. Charli crossed to the door and held it open for him. "It's late, Grant."

He stalked to the door and slammed it shut, propelling her against it. "Just for the record," he growled, "I haven't touched another woman since I started seeing you, and if you think I'm going to let you slip around behind my back, you'd damn well better think again!"

Grant captured her mouth in a possessive, almost punishing kiss, pressing her hard into the door. Her pliant breasts, crushed against his bare chest, seemed to burn him right through her stretchy pajama top. His tongue breached her closed lips, forcing them open. Holding her head still, he ravished her mouth, thrusting in a blatantly sexual rhythm. Some primal part of him needed to claim her, penetrate her, put his stamp on her. She trembled; a small whimper escaped her.

The rational part of his mind had almost managed to assert itself when he felt her hands on him, sliding up his sides. Then he was lost, his will subverted by the raw pleasure of her touch. Her mouth shifted under his, as if seeking greater contact. Her tongue stroked his, tentatively at first, then with mounting hunger. The primal, animal part of him responded, kissing her with savage intensity.

As if drawn by a magnet, Grant's hand moved to her breast. He kneaded the resilient fullness through the flimsy fabric, weighed the soft flesh in his palm. He'd only touched her through her blouse and bra before, and just that one brief time the night of their engagement. She'd been tense and unresponsive then, just tolerating his caress, or so he'd assumed. Now, as he gently plucked the erect tip, she gasped, wrenching her mouth from his. She grabbed his wrist, but didn't try to remove his hand.

Grant stared down into Charli's slumbrous eyes, which were glittering with sensual anticipation. There was no mistaking the desire he saw there. Her breathing quickened, causing her breast to nudge his palm with rhythmic insistence. Her fingers slid from his wrist to his fingers, pressing them closer, mutely urging him.

He slipped both hands under her pajama top and stroked her bare breasts. Charli's head dropped back. Grant knew he'd never heard anything as erotic as her shuddering sigh. She arched into his caress, as if offering herself, and he was helpless to resist.

He pushed her pajama top up to her shoulders. She was perfect, her breasts ample and beautifully shaped, the nipples dusky and inviting in the dim light. He bent his head and kissed one puckered tip. Charli gasped; her fingernails dug into his upper arms. He sucked the sweet, stiff peak into his mouth, and she cried out as if burned.

She was exquisitely sensitive. He suckled her greedily, teased her with his tongue and teeth, delighting in her rhythmic moans. Breathless, she gasped his name. He was wrong before, he thought distractedly. *This* was the most erotic sound—his name on Charli's lips, uttered with a desperate urgency that had his own body clamoring for release.

He claimed her other breast. She moved restlessly against him, prompting him to slide his hand down her back and under the elastic waist of her shorts. Her bottom was warm and silky under his exploring fingers, the muscles tightening as she squirmed against him with a soft exhalation. She clutched him, clung to him, and all he could think about was getting inside her.

Charli became still. Her fingertips moved lightly over his back, and he knew she felt them. The scars.

"Grant?"

Slowly he straightened, grateful for the interruption and the chance to regain control of himself, though he didn't welcome the inevitable questions.

Her eyes searched his. "Let me see." She tried to turn him, but he backed away.

"It's nothing. An old injury."

"Let me see," she repeated, stepping around him.

She had to see sooner or later, he knew. This was his home; he couldn't stay covered up forever. He stood stiffly, feeling her breath tickle the skin of his back as she simply stared. Then he felt it once more, the brush of her fingers, as light as a wisp of down.

Her voice was oddly tight. "How did this happen?"

He could lie. He'd done it before, but the thought of lying to Charli made him feel dirty. Unworthy. "It's not important." He turned to face her, ending the inspection.

"However you got those scars, I'll bet it seemed pretty important at the time."

"Drop it, Charli."

She scowled in frustration. "Why are you so secretive?" When he didn't answer, she said, "I'm your wife, Grant. We're supposed to share our past with each other, get to know what brought us to this point, what made us the way we are."

He smiled grimly. "Sometimes people are the way they are *despite* their past, not because of it." He sighed. "Listen, I told you before, I'm not withholding anything significant. That should be good enough for you."

The look on her face made him regret his words, reminding him that this entire marriage was an exercise in what was "good enough" for Charli Rossi Sterling. To his shame, that was pretty much how he'd seen it when he'd proposed. Other women held out for love, devotion and babies. But for the plain spinster schoolteacher with no other marriage prospects, just getting a prosperous, well-respected professional man's ring on her finger was "good enough." Improving her lifestyle was "good enough," more than adequate compensation for the role she was expected to play in helping him attain his goal.

Look at all she was getting out of the bargain, he'd reasoned. What right had she to complain about the lack of physical intimacy or children?

And she hadn't complained. Not one peep. She'd simply absorbed the shock of the news on their wedding night and settled in to her wifely role as dictated by her new husband.

He almost wished she'd railed and sobbed and thrown things. Then maybe he could convince himself that this really was a fair, quid pro quo arrangement, that if she wasn't content with it, she'd simply leave. Divorce him. But something told him that Charli would never leave, no matter how unhappy she was. She'd swallow her misery and tough it out.

Through an effort of will, Grant forced himself to abandon this fruitless train of thought, forced himself to focus on his goal. The snarled road map of his back was an enduring physical reminder of why, for the longest time, he'd sworn off marriage—and why, once it had become clear he couldn't achieve his goals without it, he'd orchestrated a practical, platonic union over which he could exercise complete authority.

Growing up in his turbulent childhood home, Grant had been forced to ride the out-of-control emotional roller coaster of his parents' marriage: the intoxicating, too brief highs, which inevitably bottomed out into despair, rage and violence. As a terrified child, he'd been at the mercy of their ungovernable mood swings.

Was that why he'd felt such an instant bond with Charli's family? he wondered. Why he so enjoyed spending time with them? Because they were so different from the people who'd raised him?

Perhaps he was reading too much into it. Anyone would have warmed to her family the way he had. A person would have to be made of stone not to respond to the convivial mayhem of the Rossi family get-togethers.

Mutely Charli stared at him, as if trying to read his thoughts. Finally she said, quietly, "If you change your mind—if you ever want to talk about it—I'm here."

Grant had to get out of this room, away from Charli—for all the good it would do him. The feel of her was indelibly imprinted on his hands. He tasted her still, and would continue to, he knew, as he lay in bed later, begging sleep to come.

The bleak irony was that his own wife was the last woman he should consider sharing that bed with. There was too much at stake. He'd come so far. The partnership hovered just out of reach, like a carrot on a string. It would be his, he'd vowed, before his fortieth birthday in November. He'd do whatever he had to to make it happen.

True, this expedient marriage was threatening to jump the rails, but he'd get it back on track. Of course, it would help if he could avoid intimate little encounters like this one. He never should have entered Charli's room.

Tomorrow he'd call Jayne Benning. She was sexy, uninhibited, and best of all, discreet. Knowing that within twenty-four hours he and Jayne would be a tangle of heaving bodies and sweaty limbs didn't stop him from asking, "Have there been any other men? Since you and I have been together?"

She held his gaze. "Not yet."

Grant felt an exquisite rush of relief, and that was a problem. He shouldn't care so much. After all, he couldn't argue with her reasoning. If he was free to seek sexual gratification outside their marriage, so was she.

That particular technicality hadn't occurred to him before he'd discovered that the woman he'd married was sensual, alluring and deliciously responsive. Sooner or later, she was bound to look elsewhere for what she wasn't getting at home.

Grant bade his wife a curt good-night and retreated to the solitary safety of his own room, where he punched his pillow into submission and lay staring into the dark.

There was a reason he'd married a mousy, sexless woman, damn it! So why couldn't she have stayed that way?

10

CHARLI TOOK A DEEP BREATH. "I have something to tell you."

Amanda, Sunny and Raven exchanged glances. Raven's husband, Hunter, asked, "Should I leave?"

Charli gave him a shaky smile. She shook her head. Though she hadn't known Hunter long, they'd established an instant rapport. He was almost like a brother, as encouraging and supportive as her three best friends, all of them now enjoying Sunday brunch at Hunter's comedy club, called Stitches. "No," she said, "you should hear this, too. Maybe...maybe it would help, to get a man's perspective." She took a deep breath. "Where should I start?"

Raven set down her drink, a mixture of apricot nectar and champagne. "Is it about Grant?"

Charli nodded.

"I sensed there was...a little trouble," Raven said. "I was hoping it was my imagination."

"It wasn't your imagination." Charli had agonized over the decision to confide in her lifelong pals. For the past two weeks since her wedding, she'd been too ashamed to do so. Perhaps subconsciously she'd hoped Grant would change his mind, that their marriage would miraculously turn into a normal, loving one. She now knew that if that was going to happen, she'd have to make it happen.

She stared at her plate, laden with a Greek omelette she'd barely touched. The lively sounds of Stitches buzzed around her: chatter and laughter, bluegrass music drifting from speakers, the clatter of flatware on the club's signature mismatched china. Framed antique story-magazine covers adorned the dark paneled walls. Irresistible aromas filled the air, although Charli's appetite had deserted her.

"I don't know how to say this. It'll sound so...bizarre."

A reassuring hand settled on her right shoulder—Sunny's hand.

"Our marriage is more of a...a business arrangement." Charli glanced up to gauge her friends' reactions as she continued, "We don't sleep together. There will be no children. It's the way Grant wants it. He married me to help him become partner in that stuffy law firm he works for. They don't like bachelors."

Raven and Sunny stared slack-jawed at her. Amanda muttered a string of curses under her breath. Hunter's features tightened into an angry mask. He asked, "And you agreed to this?"

"No, but...he thought I had. I mean, when he proposed, he said something about it being a, um, companionable marriage. Stuff like that. But he didn't really spell it all out. He felt bad about that, later. He thought I understood."

"Don't you dare make excuses for him!" Amanda hissed, her face blooming with angry color.

"I'm not. He just... It's complicated."

"He's using you," Sunny said miserably. She looked around the table. "And we arranged it. We introduced them."

"This isn't your fault," Hunter told them. He shoved his fingers through his dark, wavy hair, which was long enough to curl over the collar of his faded, black denim shirt. "No one could have predicted that this guy would be so completely screwed up."

Tears clogged Charli's throat. "I love him."

Amanda groaned and dropped her head into her hands.

Sunny said, "Charli, you're just confused—"

"I do," she insisted. "I've loved him since—since that first night, when he took me to dinner and that club, and—and kissed me."

It took no mental gymnastics to decipher the look that passed among her friends. *Poor, naive Charli. One kiss and she's head over heels.*

Amanda said, "I'll tell my divorce lawyer to expect your call."

"No!"

"Honey, what's the use in prolonging it?" Sunny asked. "Do you want to spend the rest of your life in a 'companionable' marriage?"

"No, but..."

"Please don't tell me you're going to change him," Amanda pleaded. "Men don't change. Period."

"Oh, I don't know," Hunter said, sliding Raven a teasing look. "You'd be surprised how a guy's priorities can get turned around, given the right incentive."

Amanda rolled her eyes. "God save me from starry-eyed newlyweds."

"You gonna eat that?" Sunny asked Hunter, reaching across the table to spear his last piece of French toast.

"So let me get this straight." Amanda lowered her voice. "You and Grant haven't had sex? Not even once?"

Charli shook her head.

"So you're still a virgin."

Charli shot a quick glance at Hunter, now contemplating a slice of bacon with undue interest. Could her face get any hotter?

"Good!" Sunny pronounced. "The bastard doesn't deserve you. Save it for somebody who does."

How could Charli make them understand? It wasn't so cut-and-dried.

The waitress arrived and took the dessert order. Everyone ordered something except Charli. "You can take this away," she said, indicating her uneaten omelette.

Hunter addressed the waitress. "Lisa, bring the lady a double espresso." When Charli started to object, he said, "A little caffeine will do you good, Carlotta. And you told me yourself the espresso we serve here is *delicioso*."

Raven, sitting on her left, placed her hand over Charli's. "Okay, so Grant married you to advance his career. He's introducing you to his colleagues, I take it?"

"Only a couple of them so far. We're giving our first formal dinner party for some of the partners in a couple of weeks. I'm a little nervous, but at least Grant gave me enough notice. He learned the hard way not to spring things on me at the last minute. I just hope I don't do anything to embarrass him."

Hunter frowned. "What makes you think you'd embarrass him?"

"Well, he's real particular about appearances—anything that can influence the big shots in his firm. He's been coaching me on etiquette, what to talk about, how to dress. Even what newspapers and magazines to read."

Amanda grumbled, "Move over, Henry Higgins."

Charli would have laughed, if the comparison between her and *My Fair Lady*'s Eliza Doolittle weren't so wretchedly accurate. As if she weren't self-conscious enough before, her husband's incessant "constructive criticism" had further eroded her confidence.

Charli brightened. "I did manage to keep my old car, though."

"Your Camry?" Sunny frowned. "What do you mean, you got to keep it?"

"Well, he wanted to buy me a new Infiniti. He was real insistent about it. But I like my car and I refused to let him replace it."

"Guess you showed him," Amanda said dryly.

Raven glared at Amanda. To Charli she said, "Good for you. You're learning to hold your own with him."

"But he won't *sleep* with her!" Amanda cried, ignoring everyone else's attempt to shush her. "Am I the only one who sees this as a major stumbling block? At least my two exes liked sex."

"Grant likes sex," Charli said. "Just not—" She clamped her mouth shut, but the others heard the part unsaid. She saw it in their faces. *Just not with me.*

"All right," Hunter snarled. A muscle jumped in his jaw. "I'm going to take this guy apart."

"He's sleeping with other women?" Amanda asked. "Well, of course he is. Stupid question."

"Let me guess," Sunny said. "He expects you to sit by the hearth darning his socks while he jumps in the sack with all these other women. What's good for the gander is off-limits to the goose."

"That might've been what he expected," Charli said, with a little smile, "before last Wednesday." She told them about her conversation with Grant, and how she'd implied that she was enjoying the same freedoms as he.

"That's my girl!" Amanda crowed.

Hunter just chuckled, a rich, deep, wickedly appreciative sound that had Charli biting back a snicker of her own. It *had* been rewarding, watching Grant's face as he began to realize there would be no double standard in their so-called marriage. His reaction had told her he wasn't as indifferent to her as he tried to pretend.

Raven was smiling, too. "What did he do?"

"He…" Charli took a deep breath and blurted, "He shoved me against the door and kissed me till I practically fainted."

Four sets of eyebrows shot up.

"And other stuff," she said.

"You let him do other stuff?" Amanda snapped.

"What other stuff?" Sunny asked.

"You know..." Charli wasn't going to say it!

"Is this where I should leave?" Hunter asked, but no one was paying any attention to him.

Amanda leaned toward Charli. "But not all the way?"

"No, I told you, I'm still..." She hesitated.

"A virgin. You can say it." Amanda leaned back so Lisa, the waitress, could set down her mug of jasmine tea. "Lord knows you've been one long enough."

Didn't Charli know it!

As the others started in on their desserts, Charli sipped her espresso and said, "I don't want you to think it's all bad. Grant is, well, he can be really sweet. I had that awful cold, you know, a couple of days after the wedding, and he took such good care of me, tucking me into bed and bringing me hot drinks and aspirin and running out to the all-night pharmacy to get me cough syrup. He didn't even care about all the germs I was exposing him to. He just wanted me to feel better."

"That's great," Sunny said, "but, honey, it doesn't nearly make up for..." She raised her hands and let them fall.

"And just yesterday he took me sailing," Charli said. "He's got this big sloop, and when he found out I'd never been sailing—can you believe it, me growing up on an island?—he took me out on the Sound. I was afraid I'd get seasick, but he put these elastic bands on my wrist with these little buttons that press on an acupuncture point, and anyway, I felt fine and we stayed out for hours and he made me take the tiller.

Me! I almost steered us into a buoy, but he was just as calm and patient as anything."

Grant had given his boat the lawyerly-sounding name *Tempus Fugit*, meaning "time flies." Its cabin consisted of two separate areas: a main room with two bench beds and basic kitchen facilities, and a two-person sleeping space in the bow. Had he ever stayed out all night in the boat? she'd asked him. His answer had been a simple yes, and she'd dropped the subject, not wanting to know how many women had shared that cozy sleeping nook with him, even if he'd been willing to tell her.

"The weird thing is," she said, "he likes kids."

Sunny looked up from her banana split. "I thought you said—"

"He doesn't *want* children—at least he doesn't want to do what gets you children—"

"With *you*," Amanda interjected, and Raven smacked her shoulder.

"But he's so good with kids," Charli continued. "You should've seen him with my one-year-old grandniece."

Sunny asked, "The Good Twin or the Evil Twin?"

"The Evil Twin."

The table erupted in a chorus of "Oohs." Everyone there had met little Valkyrie.

"So it's not that he hates kids or anything," Charli said. "The thing is, I think he feels guilty. About denying me children. And a, you know, normal marriage. He keeps buying me these expensive presents. I wish he'd stop."

Amanda opened her mouth to comment, but Raven silenced her with a look.

"I know he's given you some bitchin' jewelry," Sunny said. "The ring set for starters, and there's that emerald bracelet, too."

"And a sapphire necklace," Charli said.

"You should be wearing your stones," Amanda said. "They're not doing any good sitting at home."

Charli's smile was lopsided. "The new stuff looks out of place in my old jewelry box, the one Grandma and Grandpa Rossi gave me when I was ten. That's something else I won't let him replace."

Raven looked at Amanda, who mimed the act of zipping her mouth.

"And he's bought me all those new clothes, of course," Charli related, "but they're, I don't know, more of a costume really, to make me look presentable when we hobnob with the senior partners. When I was sick with that cold he bought me this beautiful antique trinket box with gorgeous marquetry work on the outside. Just to cheer me up. And he tried to give me a sable coat. In May! But you know I'm ethically opposed to wearing fur."

Amanda let out a strangled whimper, but swallowed back whatever choice words she had on the subject.

Raven said, "And you think these presents are his attempt to make up for all that you're giving up in your marriage?"

Charli nodded. "Yeah, I do, but I don't think he realizes that's what he's doing. It's not like a conscious thing."

"He *should* make it up to you," Amanda said. "And you should take everything he offers—right before you divorce his sorry ass."

"I don't want a divorce. At least...not yet. I want to get to know him first. There's so much about him that's still a mystery."

"Like how does he have the nerve to treat you this way," Sunny offered. "There's a mystery for you."

"He's had something really bad happen in his past, I'm sure of it, but he won't talk about it. I guess he doesn't trust me enough."

"It's not you," Hunter said. "Sounds like this guy doesn't trust anyone but himself."

"He has these..." Charli's voice shook. She lowered her voice. "He has these scars. Raised welts. On his back. It looks like...it's this crosshatch pattern, but irregular. I can't imagine what would have done that."

The others lapsed into sober silence.

"All he'd tell me is it's an old injury," Charli said. "What kind of injury would do that?"

"A car accident maybe," Sunny said.

Raven said, "With damage only to his back? It doesn't seem likely."

Hunter frowned. "Maybe he was in some kind of industrial accident."

"I don't know anything about his past except that he grew up in a small town in Pennsylvania," Charli said. "I have no idea what other kinds of jobs he might've had or anything like that."

Raven asked, "How have things been the last few days since the two of you got a little physical?"

"He's been avoiding me."

"Taking you sailing doesn't sound like avoidance," Sunny said.

"He's keeping his distance is what I mean. Even in the boat, the two of us were never inside the cabin at the same time. He made sure of that."

Hunter chuckled again. "Sounds like you've got the guy on the run."

"I don't want him on the run," Charli whined. "I want him..."

Raven said what Charli couldn't. "You want him in your bed. There's nothing wrong with that. He's your husband, Charli." She gave her a gentle smile. "That's where he belongs. And that's what you deserve."

"But she doesn't deserve a user," Sunny insisted. "And that's what this guy sounds like."

Amanda turned on Sunny. "Aren't you the one who's so eager to get married? Who's so gung ho about this whole Wedding Ring? I figured you'd be insisting Charli stick it out for the full three months, like you did with Raven."

"I just hate seeing Charli hurt. Rejected. I know what that feels like."

Charli knew Sunny was referring to her one serious relationship, way back in high school. After graduation, Kirk Larsen had gone to Stanford University in California, and Sunny had taken her waitressing job at Wafflemania. She hadn't seen him since. They'd heard that Kirk had become a physics professor.

Sunny had dated during the past twelve years, but her friends knew that she'd never felt the same way about anyone else. Charli suspected she was looking for Kirk in every man she went out with.

"Charli." Raven looked her in the eye. "Is Grant what you really want? Because I have to tell you, it doesn't sound promising."

"Yes." Charli raised her chin, practically daring anyone to take exception. "I want Grant. He's the man I married and he's the man I love."

After a thick silence, Hunter said, "I told you before, Carlotta, and I meant it. Whoever you end up with is going to be a very lucky man."

He'd told her that last month, when he'd married Raven. At the time, she'd thought he was just trying to be nice to his bride's pathetically unmarriageable friend. Now she believed him when he said he meant it.

"And if Grant doesn't straighten out," Sunny said, "we'll just find you someone else."

"My grandma said... This is kind of embarrassing," Charli murmured. "She said I should ask you guys for advice."

Amanda said, "Isn't that what we've been giving you?"

"No, I mean advice about...learning to employ my feminine wiles."

All eyes turned toward Hunter. "What?" he asked. "You want me to leave *now*, just when things are getting juicy?"

"No," Amanda said. "You're the one who's going to tell her how to make things juicier."

He looked from her face to his wife's to Sunny's. "Oh, now, wait a minute. What do I know about feminine wiles?"

"You're a man," Amanda said. "You know what works."

"Actually," Charli told Amanda, "Nonni said *you* were the expert on men."

Amanda perked up. "Your grandma said that?"

"Right before she grumbled something in Italian about your two divorces. Anyway, I know I'm a little rusty in this area, but I was starting to get the hang of it Wednesday night. I just need a few pointers."

Raven turned to her husband. "Hunter?"

He sighed and signaled the waitress. "If I'm going to do this, I'll need another drink."

11

"MIND A LITTLE COMPETITION?"

Grant looked up from the pool table to see Charli leaning in the doorway of his sprawling basement game room, which was filled with pinball machines, table hockey, table football and a jukebox—all the entertainments that other kids, kids from normal, middle-class homes, had taken for granted while growing up. Tonight he'd switched on only the large, modern chandelier hanging over the pool table, isolating it in a circle of light.

Charli hadn't changed clothes; she still had on the outfit she'd worn to dinner. Her sleeveless V-neck top was made of some clingy material in pale, opalescent pink, like the inside of a seashell. It seemed to change color with every breath. She'd paired it with a trim, plum-colored skirt short enough to expose an enticing amount of thigh. She was now barefoot, he noticed, her legs bare. She'd shed the sheer black stockings and high-heeled sandals.

Charli had gotten her hair restyled a couple of days earlier. It was just as long in back, but the front had been cut into wispy bangs that curved to softly frame her face. It was a more sophisticated, flattering style. Tonight she'd managed to coax a bit of wave out of the straight strands, so her hair had body and movement where normally it just kind of hung there. She'd also applied some makeup, with more proficiency than he'd thought her capable of—just enough to give her eyes a sultry cast, her lips a sensual pout.

They'd gone out to dinner with Mark Mahon, a partner at Grant's firm, and Mark's wife, Julie. When the four of them had entered the elegant French restaurant, heads had turned. Grant noticed male patrons subtly checking out Charli. Walking behind her, he was hard-pressed himself not to stare at her smooth, honey-colored shoulders, the subtle sway of her hips under the formfitting skirt, and especially her legs—good God, those surprisingly shapely legs, made all the more so by her high heels.

This is Charli! he'd wanted to yell, as he held her chair and intercepted yet another appreciative male glance. *Charli Rossi Sterling doesn't look like this! Not really.* If she did, he wouldn't have married her.

Dinner with the Mahons had been a chore, distracted as Grant had been by his wife's abrupt transformation into a babe. For her part, she'd comported herself admirably, conversing intelligently about current events while carefully avoiding controversial issues, laughing delightedly at Mark's lame jokes, complimenting Julie on her ugly dress and exercising impeccable table etiquette.

The Mahons had already been invited to the dinner party Grant and Charli had planned for next Saturday. Grant viewed the event as a sort of "coming out" for his bride, marking his official transformation, in the eyes of the partners, from hell-raising bachelor to stable married man. He tried not to think about how much was riding on the party. Julie asked Charli who she'd gotten to cater it.

"Oh, I'm cooking everything myself."

"For a dozen people?" Julie's overplucked eyebrows climbed toward her hairline.

"How did you persuade a gem like this to marry you?" Mark ragged Grant. "Beauty, brains, and she's talented in the kitchen."

"Don't say that until you've tasted my cooking," Charli said, with a becoming blush.

"Charli's modest," Grant said. "She's an incredible cook. But her talent isn't restricted to the kitchen. You should attend one of her concerts at Courtland High, watch her conduct her students. Those kids are amazing. How many do you have in the symphonic band, sweetheart?"

"Ninety-eight," Charli answered, regarding him with quiet intensity. His use of the endearment "sweetheart" had surprised him as much as it had her; it had just popped out. He hoped she didn't think it was a calculated ploy on his part to cast the two of them as typical lovey-dovey newlyweds. Or perhaps what had surprised her was hearing him brag about her competence as a teacher and conductor.

"The band had its spring concert last night," Grant said. "They performed this one piece that knocked my socks off. It was from the movie *Saving Private Ryan*. The band played while the concert choir sang—no lyrics, just these wonderful harmonized tones. Meanwhile they dimmed the lights and projected war-related photos on a screen."

"Sounds kind of depressing," Julie said.

"No, it was magnificent. Powerful." Grant felt a chill just remembering it. "I can state categorically that that was the first time I've ever gotten misty-eyed listening to a high school band."

Everyone laughed, and Mark teased, "Could it have been the lovely conductor who so moved you?"

Grant's only complaint about that piece was that the dim lighting obscured his view of his wife. Never before had he seen her in her formal concert attire, a tailored black tuxedo with a white pleated shirt. He knew it wasn't intended to make her look sexy, but damn if it didn't give him additional fuel for the fantasies that kept him awake half the night.

During the cake-and-coffee reception in the school's cafeteria afterward, he'd been proud to be introduced as Mrs. Sterling's new husband. The kids obviously had tremendous respect for Charli. He sensed she was tough but fair. She expected a lot out of her musically gifted students, and according to her, they rarely disappointed her.

The rest of the dinner with the Mahons had been uneventful. It was clear that Mark had been favorably impressed by Charli. He'd even taken Grant aside later to congratulate him on having made such a promising match.

Grant had secluded himself in his game room as soon as they'd returned home, hoping Charli would go straight to bed. Instead here she was, moving closer in his peripheral vision as he set up his shot. The cue tip skidded off the cue ball, which rebounded off the rail and rolled well clear of the six ball, its intended target.

"Maybe I should make a bet." Charli sat next to him on the edge of the pool table. "Doesn't look like you're too sharp tonight."

She was close enough to touch. Against his will, he breathed deeply of her familiar scent, light, soapy and thoroughly feminine. Ten days had passed since that incident in Charli's bedroom when he'd come close to losing control and sabotaging his well-laid plans. Since then, he'd scrupulously avoided a repeat performance.

It hadn't been easy. Now that he was aware of her innate sensuality, it almost seemed as if she was teasing him at every turn, although he knew that was just his sex-starved imagination working overtime.

Charli had taken to wearing only a towel, tucked low on her bosom, when sauntering from the hallway bathroom to her room after her morning shower. He supposed if he could remember to keep his own bedroom door closed, he wouldn't be distracted by the sight of her half-naked and damp, with water droplets trailing from her wet hair into her bounteous cleavage, while he held his breath waiting for the towel to succumb to the strain and pop off with her next inhalation. Clearly she was unaware of being observed from behind his half-opened door, making him feel like a voyeur.

Likewise, she'd started coming to the kitchen for breakfast and nighttime snacks wearing only those flimsy little pajamas or, worse yet, a very short nightgown under which she wore absolutely nothing. This was not guesswork on Grant's part. His powers of observation had gotten a strenuous workout during the past week or so.

That very morning Charli had stood in the breakfast nook spooning up a bowl of shredded wheat, backlit by the early morning sunlight streaming through both the bay window and her white cotton nightie. Transfixed by the sight, Grant had dribbled orange juice down his best power tie.

On one level, he was pleased that Charli no longer felt the need to bundle up in her thick, high-necked bathrobe the way she had at first. It meant she'd begun to feel comfortable and relaxed in her new home. Unfortunately, what made his wife comfortable made Grant decidedly *un*comfortable.

The worst, though, had been Monday evening, when she'd insisted on giving him a haircut, assuring him that she'd been trimming her parents' hair since she was a teenager. She'd produced her barber tools, planted him in a kitchen chair and draped him with a black nylon cape. She'd taken her time, painstakingly combing and snipping, running her cool fingers through the strands, gently blowing stray hairs off his neck, inadvertently brushing up against him. Thank God for the concealing cape, or she'd have witnessed the effect all this intimate attention had had on him.

Grant had called Jayne Benning last Thursday, as he'd promised himself he would. He'd arranged to meet her after work for cocktails in the bar of one of Manhattan's small boutique hotels, off the beaten path. There he'd bought Jayne her usual vodka gimlet and tossed back two stiff bourbons while trying to mentally psych himself up for the elevator ride up-stairs to the room he'd already reserved.

In the end the room had gone unused. He'd shared with Jayne the news of his recent marriage, told her how great it was to see her again, given her a brisk peck on the cheek and hailed the bewildered woman a taxi.

Grant could no longer blame his dormant sex life on wedding preparations or long hours at the firm or any of the other excuses he'd concocted during the past few weeks. He was forced to acknowledge his increasing distaste for the idea of cheating on his wife.

But it's not cheating! the rational part of him argued. He and Charli both knew what kind of marriage they had. He should feel no hesitation about pursuing outside relationships.

Neither should she, the nagging voice continued, leaving him half convinced that if he refrained from exercising his right to make whoopee, so might Charli. Didn't make any sense, but he couldn't help that.

Grant stepped away from Charli and moved around the table, closer to the cue ball. He struggled to concentrate on his next shot.

She asked, "Did I do something wrong at dinner?"

He looked up. "No. What makes you say that?"

"You've been kind of quiet ever since we left the restaurant."

"You were fine at dinner, Charli. Terrific, actually."

"It was sweet of you to say those nice things about me and my students and all."

"I meant them. You know that. And to be honest, it kind of irked me that we'd been talking with the Mahons for, what, about an hour at that point, and neither of them had asked you anything about your job."

She shrugged. "I sort of expected that."

"It was rude. It was almost like they saw you as nothing more than an extension of me."

He half expected her to say, *Well, aren't I?* After all, he'd made it excruciatingly clear from the beginning that their marriage was about his career.

Instead she said, "That briefcase you gave me after the concert is, well, it's just gorgeous, but you shouldn't have."

"You always say that. I never met a woman who so disliked receiving gifts."

"I don't dislike them, Grant, they're just...not necessary. Not for every little occasion. Really, you spoil me."

At times like this, Grant wanted to shake Charli. Considering all that his wife was required to forgo in her marriage, why on earth should she do without what he *could* give her?

"This was a special concert for you," he said. "I could've given you a bouquet, but flowers die. And I knew you could use a new briefcase. That ratty old thing you were carrying around was about to split at the seams."

"Well, thank you again, but—"

"Don't say it. Anyway, as for tonight, you really were terrific with Mark and Julie. I was surprised."

"Were you?"

"Maybe *surprised* isn't the right word," he said, bridging the cue on his knuckles and sinking the six ball. "I have faith in you, Charli. I hope you realize that."

"Faith in my ability to help you make partner?"

He looked up at her then. Was that a trace of bitterness he heard?

She hopped off the table and selected a cue from the nearby wall rack. "Are you just fooling around here or would you care for a game of eight ball?"

He gestured in invitation. "I'm just sinking balls. Be my guest." Now that she was here, he couldn't exactly kick her out.

She circled the table, chalking her cue, staring at the dozen balls remaining on the table. "Because that's what this is all about, isn't it?" she asked. "You making partner."

Charli was across from him now, leaning over the table, taking aim with her cue. She seemed oblivious to the fact that the V neckline of her pink top gaped open, exposing lush breasts barely corralled by a silver lace-and-satin bra. Grant wasn't concerned about being caught staring. She was concentrating fixedly on the balls before her.

"I was just wondering," she said, sliding the cue back and forth in preparation for her shot. Back and forth again. Why had Grant never noticed how blatantly sexual that was? "If your making partner is the purpose of our marriage, what happens after you achieve that goal?" She hit the cue ball with a smart crack, sinking the eleven ball in the corner pocket. She looked up at him, awaiting an answer.

"My making partner isn't the sole purpose of our marriage."

"It isn't?"

"Not anymore. Although without question it was the, uh, instigating factor." He gave a wry smile. "Please don't tell me how lawyerly I sound."

"I wouldn't dream of it," she said dryly. "Does this mean our *arrangement* won't end once you become a partner?"

"Are you talking about divorce? Charli, I have no intention of divorcing you."

"What if you don't make partner?" Staring levelly at him, she added, "It could happen, married or not. You have to be prepared for that."

"I know there are no guarantees," he said gruffly. "I'm just trying to give myself an edge."

"Well, what if all this doesn't work?" She spread her arms, indicating herself, the two of them. "I'm thinking I've got forty or fifty years of your resentment to look forward to, if that should happen."

"Why would I resent *you*?"

"Come on. You saddled yourself with an unwanted wife for one purpose only. Maybe the senior partners won't be so impressed by me. Maybe they'll see through the ploy. Maybe they just won't offer you a partnership and it'll have nothing to do with your marital status. But you'll still be stuck with me."

Grant had heard little after "unwanted wife." He gripped his cue so hard his knuckles were white. "I never said I didn't want you, Charli. Ours may not be a conventional marriage, we may not have those kinds of feelings for each other, but...I want you. I want you by my side."

"Even if you don't make partner."

He tried to smile. "Let's hope that doesn't become an issue."

Charli wasn't smiling. She waited for an answer.

"Even if I don't make partner," he said. The truth was, he'd gotten used to having Charli around. He couldn't imagine living alone again in this big house.

Grant examined the pool table and targeted the three ball. As he lined up the difficult shot, Charli said, "You never ask me to join you down here for pool or table football or anything anymore."

She had to know why. "We don't have to spend all our free time together."

After a moment she said, "Should I leave?"

His fingers tightened on the cue. "I didn't mean you aren't welcome down here, Charli. This is your home, too."

"I guess I don't really feel that way yet."

He made his shot, tapping the cue ball into the seven ball, watching it bump the three ball into the side pocket. He straightened. "It'll take time. You'll adjust."

"Will you?"

"What do you mean?"

"Well, sometimes you seem a little...territorial," she said. "I can understand why. This place has been yours alone for four years. It can't be easy having someone else move in, disrupting things."

"You haven't disrupted anything."

Charli laughed. "You haven't given me a chance!"

"What have you wanted to do that I wouldn't let you? You haven't suggested any changes around here."

"And if I had? Be honest."

Grant wanted to refute what she was saying, but the words wouldn't come. Chagrined, he said, "Maybe I've been a little..."

"Set in your ways?" At least she was smiling.

Charli moved to his side of the table, eyeing the remaining balls.

"You know, when we got engaged," she said, "and you told me that you were set in your ways, you acknowledged that perhaps I was, as well. Think I can sink the nine ball in the corner pocket?"

"Uh, yeah. Put a little English on it. Hit it right there." He pointed to a spot on the side of the nine ball. "Listen, Charli, I know where you're going with this. You want me to let you make more decisions around here."

"No."

"What then?"

"I don't want you to *let* me do anything," she said. "I shouldn't have to ask permission."

"That's not what I meant."

"You once told me our marriage was a partnership of equals." She leaned over the table, bridged her cue. "That's what I always thought marriage was supposed to be."

"*Our* kind of marriage, yes."

She looked up at him. "Any kind of marriage. It doesn't have to be some kind of dry business transaction for both spouses to be equal partners."

"Is that how you see what we have? As a dry business transaction?"

"Wasn't that your intention?" She took her shot,

and missed. The nine ball ricocheted off the corner, skirting the pocket by a hair. When he failed to answer, she faced him squarely. "In an equal partnership, one partner doesn't control all the money and expenditures. In an equal partnership, one partner doesn't try to remold the other one into some kind of damn Stepford wife." She smiled. "*Now* do you see where I'm going with this?"

Grant was stunned; he'd never heard Charli swear. "I told you before, I'm just trying to help you—"

"Adjust. I know. Has it occurred to you that only one of us seems to be doing any adjusting around here?"

Only one of us needs *to do any adjusting,* he wanted to say, but wisely held his tongue. He directed his attention to the pool table and the four ball, which called for a tricky bank shot.

"If I needed so much adjustment," she continued, "why did you marry me? Oh, I remember now. I'm so modest and undemanding."

Had he really described her that way? Grant felt a prickle of shame, recalling their conversation on their wedding night.

"What are you doing here?" he'd demanded. "We talked about this...the kind of marriage this will be."

Charli had sat on his bed in that sheer, sexy negligee, hunched miserably with her arms around her knees, as if trying to shield herself from her husband's view. Modest and undemanding, he had indeed called her. And good-natured. He could have been describing the perfect lapdog.

Her attire tonight couldn't be called modest, although it was far •from indecent. As for being un-demanding—it would appear she'd gotten over it.

Grant hit the cue ball, banking it off the rail. It rolled harmlessly a good two inches from the four ball. Charli stood very close to him now. The overhead chandelier molded her features in a dramatic play of light and shadow, making her cheekbones higher, her mouth fuller, more prominent. Her dark eyes glittered, and Grant couldn't help but observe that indignation looked good on Charli.

He propped his cue against the table. "It would seem that first impressions can be deceiving." His fingertips brushed the bare skin above her neckline as he lifted her lustrous freshwater-pearl necklace, which matched her delicate drop earrings. Amanda had helped her choose these pieces, as well as the outfit she now wore, a couple of days earlier. This jewelry wasn't nearly as valuable as the emeralds and sapphires he'd given her, but it looked stunning against her olive complexion.

Slowly he released the necklace, letting the backs of his fingers linger on her satiny skin. Charli watched him without expression, even as her heart fluttered under his knuckles. After a moment she stepped away and scanned the pool table; her gaze zeroed in on the four ball Grant had failed to sink. For the second time, he watched her skirt inch up her bare thighs and stretch taut over her fanny as she bent at the waist. He found himself silently slipping behind her, close but not touching, prey to the inescapable tug of pure male instinct.

Sighting along her cue, Charli shifted her weight

backward and bumped up against Grant. She started to recoil from the unexpected contact, but he seized her hips and leaned into her, pressing her to the table. She looked over her shoulder at him, and something in his expression made her eyes go wide.

She dropped the cue and tried to lever herself up. He pushed on the back of her neck, pressing her flat to the table.

"Grant...!"

"You're doing it on purpose, aren't you?" He slid his free hand down her side and over her hip. "I thought no, it couldn't be, not Charli, not my timid, *modest* little bride."

Something in his tone alarmed her. She struggled to rise, briefly, and collapsed onto the table, breathing hard. Her color was high under the glare of the chandelier, her cheek pressed to the green felt. He brushed her disheveled hair off her face. She tried to look at him, but his fingers tightened fractionally on her neck, thwarting her.

"Grant," she said, breathless, "what are you doing?"

"You've been deliberately teasing me. For days now," he accused, grinding slowly against her, forcing her to acknowledge the result of her actions. "Admit it."

"Let me up."

"Isn't this what you wanted?" He pried her legs apart with his own, making her skirt ride up even higher. "To push me over the edge? Make me lose control?"

"No!" She attempted to wrench away from him, to

close her legs. Every little movement sent darts of pleasure through him.

"I don't believe you." He shoved her skirt up to her waist. She cried out, trying to buck him off of her. "These are new, aren't they?" he asked, fondling her sweet, round bottom through silver lace-and-satin bikini panties that matched the bra he'd glimpsed earlier.

"Grant, stop it!" Charli reached behind her to pull her skirt down. He easily shackled both her wrists in one hand and held them at her waist.

He'd seen the utilitarian undies his wife normally wore, folded in neat stacks in the laundry room: full-coverage white cotton underpants and bras.

"Why did you buy these," he asked, "if you didn't want me to see them? Or did you have someone else in mind at the time?" Jealousy was a poison-tipped spear, jabbing at him. To his dismay, the idea of Charli trying to subvert their platonic marriage was preferable to her sharing herself with another man.

Charli's eyes narrowed. "It's none of your damn business if I did."

"Another 'damn.' That's twice in one night." He hooked his fingers over the top edge of the panties as if to pull them down.

She gasped and went rigid. *"Don't!"*

Grant stopped, trying to reconcile days' worth of come-hither cues with Charli's obvious distress now. He kneed her legs farther apart, drinking in the enticing spectacle before him, grappling with his rampant hunger. He pressed his hand directly between Charli's legs, over the flimsy panties. A strangled cry erupted from her. Her thighs quivered as she fought to close them. He tightened his grip on her wrists.

Her heat penetrated his fingers; he stroked her slowly, exploring her intimate flesh through the thin barrier of satin. "I'm going to take you like this," he said. "A quickie on the pool table."

"No." Her voice quavered. "Grant, don't."

"Why not? It's what you want. Or do you get your kicks just teasing the hell out of me?" He continued to caress her, lightly, rhythmically. "Answer me, Charli."

"This isn't what I wanted."

"You didn't want sex?" He restated the question, using coarse language that made her flinch.

"No." In a ragged whisper she added, "I wanted you to make love to me."

Grant cursed. "You have to put it up there on some lofty plane, don't you? Does that help you keep from feeling dirty about it? Pretending that it's more than horniness, more than a basic animal need?"

"It *is* more. I couldn't do it otherwise."

"How noble." And still he stroked her. "You're wet, Charli. That's not love, it's hormones."

"Please…" she panted, obviously close to climax. "Not like this."

"It can't be any other way." He released her wrists. The sound of his belt leather sliding free of the buckle galvanized her. She twisted away from him, sliding shakily off the pool table as she yanked her skirt down.

Her voice was flat, final. "No." She gripped the edge of the table, her chest heaving.

Frustration boiled within him. "I'm willing to finish what you started."

"Do you love me?"

Grant's entire body throbbed in time to his heart-beat. "This isn't about love. Damn it, Charli. If I'd known you'd do this..."

Her chin rose. "You wouldn't have married me? It's okay, you don't have to answer. The fact is, I *do* love you, Grant. And I know you feel something for me."

With jerky movements he refastened his belt.

"Why are you so terrified of those feelings?" she asked. "Why do you push me away?"

"It didn't have to be like this." He shook his head, wondering how he'd let things get so out of hand. "We could've stuck to the game plan. *You* could've stuck to the game plan. You've known from the beginning what the deal is."

"What happened to you, Grant? What made you so afraid to let me close?" She followed him to the foot of the stairs. "Talk to me. Please. I love—"

"No, you don't!" He raised his hands, as if to ward her off. "You've convinced yourself. Go out and get laid, Charli. That's all you need. Just don't tell me about it."

12

"WHEN ARE THE SERVING people getting here?" Grant asked.

"I told you, at seven." Charli saw him check his watch, for the umpteenth time, as she stuffed the last of several dozen mushroom caps with a mixture of sautéed shallots, prosciutto, béchamel sauce and freshly grated Parmesan cheese. "You're going to be a basket case by the time everyone gets here. Calm down, Grant. Everything's under control."

He peered at the stuffed mushrooms arranged on a baking pan. "They're not uniform in size."

"Close enough. And who cares, anyway? These *funghi ripieni* are delicious. I've never had a complaint. Oh, well, except that one time..." She chewed back a smile.

Grant looked up in alarm. "What time? What happened?"

Charli laughed; she couldn't help it. "Have you ever entertained before?" She wiped her hands on her bib apron and pulled a length of plastic wrap off the roll.

"Of course I have. It's just that tonight is—"

"Important. Yes, I believe you mentioned something about that." Charli knew she should be more sympathetic, but Grant had been driving her crazy the

past few days, fixating on every little detail of tonight's dinner party, from her menu choices to the decor to the dishes and table linens. He'd insisted on
splurging on a new set of Wedgwood bone china,
ivory with a platinum rim, even though there was a
nearly new set of Russian china in the sideboard.
Charli and Grant both loved the Russian dishes, with
their bold design in cobalt blue, but they weren't suitable for this crowd, he'd insisted. Better to play it safe
with something more sedate, more conservative, more
suitable to a partner of Farman, Van Cleave and
Holm.

Charli slid the mushrooms into the built-in, Sub-
Zero refrigerator, clad in pale maple to blend in with
the kitchen decor. She had to shove aside the Jerusalem artichoke and spinach salad to make room for
them.

"I'm still not sure about that stew," Grant said, dog-
ging her steps as she pulled off the apron and tossed it
onto the butcher-block work island. The first time
Charli had laid eyes on this enormous, opulent
kitchen, she could only gape in wonder. Though the
appliances, amenities and storage were state of the art,
the room had a vintage 1940s look reminiscent of an
old diner, with its subway-tile backsplashes, glass cab-
inet doors, seafoam-green granite countertops and
lavish use of blond wood and stainless steel.

The narrow, cramped kitchen in her parents' house
looked vintage, too, but not on purpose. If avocado-
colored appliances and fat-fruit wallpaper ever came
back in style, her folks would be ready.

Charli needed a nice relaxing bath. No, she needed

a nice relaxing *bubble* bath. She deserved it. It was now midafternoon, and she'd been on her feet since the morning, cooking, laying out all the serving pieces they'd need, setting the dining table, arranging liquor and mixers on the bar in the den. Grant had hired a couple of people from a local agency to serve and clean up, but Charli had insisted on doing all the cooking herself.

He followed her out of the kitchen to the curving staircase. "I said I'm still not sure about—"

She wheeled on him. "It's *spezzatino di vitello alla salvia*—veal stew with sage and white wine, not some glop from a can, for heaven's sake."

"I know that, but—"

"It's delicious—you said so yourself."

"It's incredible, but I'm just worried that it may be a little, ah, prosaic for this kind of affair. I mean, we're serving all these other elegant dishes, and then giving them *stew* for a main course?"

Sighing, Charli trudged upstairs, with Grant right behind her. She knew he was anxious about this dinner, but her patience was wearing thin. "I told you, Grant, there's no main course. This is an Italian-style dinner. The veal stew is the *second* course, and I chose it because I could make it yesterday, and heat it up right before it's served. With everything else I'm making that has to be done at the last minute, it was the perfect choice. Tastes better the second day, anyway. Don't worry, I'll call it *spezzatino*," she said dryly. "We'll fool everyone."

Charli was in her room now, grabbing her pink terry robe. She hadn't walked around in only a towel since Grant had nearly taken her virginity on the pool table, a week ago today. She *had* been teasing him, as he'd accused, deliberately trying to goad a response out of him. She'd put all the advice she'd gotten from her friends and Hunter to good use, and even let Amanda take her clothes shopping; the outfit she'd worn to dinner with the Mahons had received Amanda's seal of approval.

For a week and a half, she'd flaunted her body in the privacy of their home, "accidentally" brushing up against her husband on numerous occasions, in an effort to force him to acknowledge his feelings for her. In the end, the only thing he'd been willing to acknowledge—to himself or to her—was a base sexual attraction. The encounter in the game room had careened out of control, leaving her shaken. During the week that had elapsed since then, they'd walked on eggs around each other, every interaction marked by a polite reserve that left her more heartsick and frustrated than ever.

The day after the pool-table incident, Grant had presented her with a gold Movado watch—as some sort of apology, she assumed.

He followed her to the spacious guest bathroom and watched as she ran water in the tub and poured in vanilla-scented bubble bath. "I just want everything to go off without a hitch."

"It will."

"I know there must be something we haven't thought of."

"I'm sure there is." His expression told her it wasn't the answer he'd been hoping for. "Did it occur to you that you might actually try to relax and enjoy your own party?"

"You're taking this whole thing so lightly."

"Lightly? Grant, I've worked my tail off for this dinner. The planning, the shopping, the cooking—"

"I know you have, and I really appreciate it. It's just that you don't seem to understand how much is riding on this, on the success of this evening."

Vanilla-scented steam wafted from the tub, quickly filling with water and froth. Charli kicked off her moccasin-style flats. She pulled the hair tie off the end of her braid and finger-combed the strands. "You're going to be so uptight it'll rub off on our guests."

"Did Sarah Holm solve her baby-sitter problem?"

"You only get to ask any question three times. After that, I ignore it." Charli started unbuttoning her blouse. "I'm going to take my bath now, so unless you'd care to scrub my back, this conversation is over."

He had to know it was just her exasperation speaking; they'd scrupulously kept their distance from each other for the past week. Nevertheless, at that moment Grant looked tempted to take her up on the offer. Charli's heart did a drumroll. In the next instant he stepped out of the room and shut the door.

Even then his fretting didn't stop. "I'm not sure about the music we chose," he called through the closed door. "I thought maybe I'd put a little more classical stuff into the mix. What do you think?"

Charli finished shedding her clothes and deposited them in the hamper.

"Charli?"

She stepped into the steaming tub and lowered herself with a sigh of contentment.

"Because I think we need to keep it more sedate," he said. "I've got that new Pachelbel CD."

She saturated her bath sponge and drizzled warm water on her throat and chest.

"Charli, are you going to answer me?"

She sank lower in the water, smiling at the dark mutterings that drifted from the other side of the door. Finally there was blessed silence.

HOW DID WOMEN GET INTO these things? For five minutes Charli had struggled in vain to fasten her new bustier, a strapless corset with boning and underwire cups that ended just above her navel. It was made of some sheer taupe material embroidered with delicate ivory flowers. Matching ivory scallop trim adorned the edges of both the bustier and the matching high-cut panties. The panties, she'd had no trouble getting into. But the stupid bustier...!

She tried to look over her shoulder in the full-length standing cheval mirror in the corner of her room, while contorting her arms behind her to attach the myriad tiny hook-and-eye closures that ran up the stretchy back. In the store's fitting room, Amanda had fastened it for her, in about two seconds. Charli hadn't considered that she wouldn't be able to get the darn thing on without a lady's maid!

She bent slightly at the waist, grappling with a hook and eye. Her hair—freshly washed and blown—fell over her eyes, obscuring her vision. Still, she managed to secure a few of the lower hooks before realizing that the sides didn't match up.

Charli shrieked in frustration, yanking at the hooks. The door quaked as Grant rapped on it a couple of times.

"Charli, what's going on?"

"I can't do this, damn it!" she cried from under all that hair.

"What's the prob—" Grant broke off.

The clarity and volume of his voice told Charli there was no longer a door between them. Her head whipped up; she shoved her hair off her face, clutching the bustier to her chest. He stood frozen, staring.

"I can't *do* this!" She actually stamped her foot. "How do women *do* this! It's—it's impossible to fasten this damn thing alone!"

Vaguely she was aware of the spectacle she presented, half-naked, flushed and breathless from her struggles, with her hair going every which way. But at the moment frustration had her close to tears, overriding all else.

Her distress finally spurred Grant into motion. He closed the distance between them and placed his hands on her bare shoulders, urging her to turn around. "Let's see."

Obediently she faced the mirror. His fingertips grazed her back as he lifted her hair out of the way. He stood a full head taller than she, and as he studied the bustier's fastenings, she saw in the mirror that his hair was wet, combed back off his face. Her nose detected the woodsy-scented soap he used, and under it, the fragrance that was his alone—the clean, stirring musk of his skin. She was reminded of that one other time he'd stood behind her at a mirror, after the twins' party, when she'd first exercised those rusty feminine wiles, brushing her hair while casually assuring her husband she'd be as discreet as he in her sexual liaisons.

Late afternoon sunlight streamed through the sheer, honey-colored curtains, gilding their figures. Only now, as he bent his head to his task, as his warm fingers linked the bottommost hook, did Charli realize Grant was in as much a state of dishabille as she. He wore only white cotton boxer shorts and one black sock. Her cry of exasperation must have caught him in the middle of dressing.

Bending closer, he squinted. "Do they have to make these things so small?"

"It's your eyes," she said. "You're pushing forty."

Without looking up he said, "I could leave now. I don't have to take this abuse."

"Fine with me. Amanda thought this bustier would be just the thing under that dress—" Charli nodded toward the bed, and the short navy cocktail dress laid out on the white, eyelet-trimmed bedspread "—but I don't have to wear anything at all underneath. Mr. Farman, Mr. Van Cleave and Mr. Holm won't mind, I'm sure."

"I'm sure." Grant's voice was a dangerous rumble. Though his breath was hot on her back, Charli shivered. "You're going to have to give up your death grip on this thing if you want me to finish doing it up."

Charli looked down to see her arms tightly locked over her chest. She loosened her hold and adjusted her breasts in the garment's cups, quickly, discreetly—but not discreetly enough, she realized, as Grant's gaze briefly swerved from the hooks to the mirror.

He said, "Why didn't you fasten it in front and then turn it around?" He'd progressed halfway up the bustier. It must be her imagination, Charli thought, but she could swear his fingers were slowing.

"I tried. This thing's too tight, and I'm too..." She didn't say it—*too big on top*—but his slow grin told her she didn't have to.

"Not too," he said, still staring at the hooks. "Just right."

The way he said it made a warm prickle crawl up Charli's body. As Grant patiently fastened the remaining hooks, she watched her "just right" breasts gradually fill the bustier's cups and swell over their scalloped tops like rising bread dough. She was unaccustomed to the snugness of the garment, the stiff boning. With every breath she felt invisible hands holding her, shaping her. Offering her.

Charli looked up to see Grant staring at her in the mirror. Again she crossed her arms over her chest, where the dusky coins of her nipples were just visible beneath the filmy taupe fabric. Grant reached around her and gently pulled her arms away, loosely holding them across her middle. His eyes were a dark gray-green.

"I've seen you, remember?" he murmured.

He'd seen her, yes, but not in unforgiving daylight, and not in a garment so blatantly sexual she felt more vulnerable than if she were naked. His hands seemed to generate some kind of electric current as they glided up her arms, finally settling on her shoulders. His head dipped and he nuzzled her hair just over her ear. All at once, air was a precious commodity. In the mirror, she watched her lips part, her nostrils flare. Her breasts rose and fell in a heightened rhythm.

As if drawn by the movement, Grant's long fingers slid lower over her chest. Dizzy, Charli let her eyes drift shut as he slowly stroked the exposed upper slopes of her breasts. Her skin was almost unbearably sensitive. She felt her nipples pull into stiff knots, and knew without opening her eyes that he was watching it happen.

His words were a scalding whisper against her scalp. "How could I have ever thought..." With a ragged sigh, he pressed a kiss to her hair. "You're more woman than I ever could have imagined. God, I must've been blind. Or crazy. Maybe both."

His hands moved downward over her breasts. Charli's breath caught at the shock of pleasure that arrowed from the aching tips straight to the feminine heart of her. She opened her eyes and watched her husband's big hands progress down the stiff front of the bustier, over the band of exposed skin where her belly button peeked out. They settled on either side of her hips, his long, splayed fingers nearly meeting over the dark triangle clearly visible through her panties.

Breathless, Charli watched Grant's hands shift to frame the triangle between his thumbs and fingers. Tingling warmth flooded her intimate flesh. She felt heavy down there, needy. In her ear he whispered, "Do you touch yourself here? In your bed at night?"

She grasped his wrists, shocked by the question,

mortified that he could guess how deeply she hungered, here, in the cloistered hell of this beautifully appointed bedroom.

"Answer me, Charli." He met her eyes in the mirror. His hands moved a little, up and down, in a slow, seductive cadence, close to but not touching the place that so desperately needed to be touched. "You do, don't you?"

Sharp-edged craving battled with Charli's anger and resentment. She tried to pull his hands away, but they were immovable. "So what if I do," she snapped. "Don't you?"

The corners of his eyes crinkled, the only hint of a smile. "More than I did when I was a teenager, thanks to you." He seized her hand and slipped it under the top edge of her panties. "Show me what you do, Charli." He kissed her temple, his eyes still on hers; he stroked her fingers through the panties in a suggestive rhythm. "Show me how you pleasure yourself."

"No." She struggled without success to extricate her hand.

"I've imagined you doing it," he said. "I've pictured you raising your nightgown, parting your legs..."

"Did you ever picture *yourself* raising my nightgown, parting my legs?"

His fingers tightened on hers; his voice was low and hoarse. "Charli, I've pictured myself doing everything to you that you could possibly imagine." He smiled grimly. "And a few things I'll bet you couldn't."

He released her hand, only to replace it with his own, sliding his fingers down her belly and under her panties. She stiffened, and he soothed her with his gentle touch, with the low, rich timbre of his voice as he murmured hotly in her ear.

Charli stared, spellbound, as Grant's hand moved lower, as his fingertips parted the springy curls. She trembled, clinging to his other arm, now clamped around her waist. He watched her in the mirror, his gaze darker, more intense, than she'd ever seen it. His fingers curled inward, touched the slippery folds. Charli gasped, barely aware of her nails digging into his arm.

He emitted a groan of pure male satisfaction, exploring further as if to test her wetness, her readiness. He found her most sensitive spot, holding her tighter still as she arched against the fiery burst of sensation. Languidly he stroked her, until her breathing matched the cadence of his caress, until her body rocked in time to it. It was as if everything outside the two of them had ceased to exist.

She barely recognized the woman in the mirror, with her slumbrous eyes and her tousled hair and the flush of passion sweeping from breasts to hairline. Her breath caught as one long finger pushed into her, a short distance only before he paused.

"Charli?" Grant's eyebrows drew together. His finger probed gently. He looked down at her then, not at the mirror, but at *her*. "It can't be..." he breathed.

Charli didn't even try to make sense of his words, overcome by the glut of pleasure, the unaccustomed feeling of being caressed from within. Mindlessly she pushed against his hand.

He pressed his lips to her hair, closed his eyes

briefly. "Charli, sweetheart, tell me. Have you ever been with a man?"

Why was he asking that? He had to know the answer. "Grant," she moaned, and reflexively pressed her hand over his, through the thin fabric of her panties. Slowly his finger burrowed deeper. Charli shuddered, and uttered his name again, a tortured plea.

Transfixed, she watched the rhythmic movement of his hand in the mirror, felt the pumping, clutching response of her body. The hunger coiled hotter, tighter, until release shimmered at the edges of her awareness, like gasoline fumes needing only a random spark to ignite.

For an instant, Charli panicked—she'd never shared this with anyone. Grant seemed to sense her hesitation. "Don't fight it," he whispered in her ear. "Give yourself to it, that's right, that's it, sweetheart, you're so beautiful...."

At the critical moment, he deepened his caress and her orgasm detonated, a fireball of sensation that she greeted with a hoarse shout. Her eyes squeezed shut and her world shrank to the pulsating pleasure that went on and on as Grant continued to stoke it.

Awareness gradually returned, like sunshine burning away fog. Her eyes drifted open and she saw herself in the mirror, drowsy and limp, supported by her husband's long, powerful arms. He slid his hand out of her panties, now damp with her passion. Reality crashed in on her, bringing with it a sense of loss.

"Don't let that be all," she pleaded, shameless in her need now that she'd had a taste of the fulfillment they were meant to share.

"Charli..." Tenderly he turned her in his arms.

"Don't say it shouldn't have happened." Tears pricked her eyes. "I couldn't bear that."

"Shh...sweetheart." His lips touched hers, lightly but with a depth of feeling that startled her. Nevertheless, she felt the tension in his body, and braced herself for the words that would break her heart. *This meant nothing,* he would tell her. *It won't happen again.*

But Grant didn't say those things. He just stared at Charli, studying her, as if he'd never seen her before. "You're a virgin," he said at last.

"Of course. What did you think?"

His expression went from awestruck to chagrined. "I didn't think, I assumed."

"But you...well, you had to know I'm not experienced. Men haven't exactly been beating down my door all these years."

His hands slid around her back. Quietly he said, "Charli, if you reached the three-decade mark untouched, it's not because you're unattractive, or undesirable."

She averted her face; he turned it back, making her look at him, at his lopsided smile. "Which you're *not*, no matter how much you may have convinced yourself." The smile faded. "No matter how much I may have made you feel that way. If I did... God, I didn't mean to. Please believe that."

Charli swallowed hard, torn between her stubborn pride—*don't be silly, I've always known I'm nothing special, why should the truth bother me?*—and her bone-deep need to have the man she loved appreciate her, admire her. Want her.

Looking into her eyes, he stated the simple truth. "It was your choice. You waited for marriage."

"I waited for *you*," Charli whispered, forcing the words past the knot in her throat.

A look of such shining, unadulterated wonder came into Grant's eyes that they seemed to glow from within, glistening with emotion. "Want to hear something funny?" He brushed her tangled hair off her face. "I thought the reason you refused to sleep with me back when we were dating was that you suffered from some kind of deficient libido." With a self-deprecating smirk he added, "I mean, what else could've made you immune to my raw sex appeal?"

"I wanted to," Charli admitted. "I just...didn't show it. I didn't want you to know I had those feelings. It seems so foolish now."

"Sweetheart, when it comes to foolishness, I think I take the prize." He lifted her into his arms and walked toward her bed.

Her eyes grew wide; she clung to his shoulders. "What are you doing?"

Grant set her down on the white bedspread. He lifted the cocktail dress off the bed and draped it over the back of her dressing-table chair. "We've talked enough."

13

CHARLI'S HEART BUCKED against her rib cage. She watched Grant pull off his one black sock. She watched him drop his boxer shorts and kick them away.

Then she could only stare wide-eyed. Nothing had prepared her for the sight of her husband naked and thoroughly aroused. He was magnificent, perfectly proportioned and smoothly muscled. Every part of him was beautiful, including that most mysterious part now revealed to her. That part was beautiful and potent and, good heavens, enormous.

"Don't tell me you're having second thoughts," he said with a small smile, never taking his eyes off her face. He joined her on the bed, pushing her down and lying next to her, propped on an elbow.

"I...no, of course not." Charli swallowed hard. "I just didn't expect... I've never seen..."

He lifted her hand and placed it on his rigid penis. After a stunned instant she lightly wrapped her fingers around him. He was smooth and hot and impossibly hard, and he twitched under her touch. Grant's features softened; he made a little sound, half sigh, half moan. His long fingers enfolded hers and he showed her how to caress him, with light, rhythmic pressure.

"It's hard to believe..." she said, watching him grow even larger. "I mean, is this really going to...?"

She felt rather than heard his chuckle. "Sweetheart, I have a feeling we're going to fit like we were made for each other." He sobered, and lifted her hand from his rampant flesh, twining his fingers with hers. He looked directly into her eyes. "I need you to trust me, Charli. I'll be as careful as I know how."

"It's okay. I know...I know it'll hurt. The first time."

"Maybe the second and third times a little, too," he said, reinforcing what she already knew—that Grant was a man of experience, a fact both comforting and daunting. How could she ever catch up, learn to please him? How could she ever compete with the sophisticated women he was accustomed to?

He raised her fingers to his lips, placed a warm kiss on her knuckles, his gaze still boring into hers. Charli lowered her eyes, half convinced he could read her mind.

"You're all I've thought about," he murmured, releasing her hand to trail his fingers over the exposed tops of her breasts. "Not an hour goes by that I don't imagine stripping you naked and taking you, right there, wherever I happen to be at the moment." His lips quirked. "I've had you under my favorite table at the Four Seasons, and in my car—front seat and back—and everywhere in the game room, and about a hundred times on my desk at work. Oh, and once we did it in Judge Randolph's chambers. Sometimes I imagine I can smell you, your soapy scent, and that's all it'll take to get me instantly hard."

He stroked his hand down her side to her hip.

"Charli, you're the most fascinating woman I've ever known. I haven't wanted anyone else since I met you. Hell of a playboy I am, obsessing about my wife."

An *obessione*. Nonni had been right, Charli thought. Grant *had* been looking at her like that, thinking about her like that. She touched his cheek, clean-shaven for the party. She slid her fingers around to his nape, pulled him down and claimed his lips.

This was a greedy kiss, hot and openmouthed and urgent. Charli didn't stop to wonder if she was doing it right; she didn't care how brazen or demanding she appeared. She *felt* brazen. She *felt* demanding. For once, she let herself go, satisfying her own clamoring desires, with no thought to propriety or ladylike behavior.

Grant's groan of startled pleasure fueled her passion. They writhed like animals in heat, clung to each other with arms and legs and hard, hungry mouths. She wrestled for position, angling herself on top of him, only to have him roll her underneath him with one sinewy burst of speed.

The weight of him pressing her into the mattress triggered a dizzying rush of heat. The pressure of his big body, the leashed power of him, aroused her unbearably. Restlessly she moved underneath him. He leaned more heavily into her, pinning her with both his strength and his penetrating gaze. An unspoken communication flowed between them, ancient and immutable. For all their civilized trappings, they were still, beneath it all, as nature made them.

Charli held her husband's gaze for long moments, as the old alarm clock on her dresser ticked and the breeze billowed the sheer curtains, bringing with it the green scents of spring. Finally she flexed her hips upward, slowly, deliberately. She felt an insistent presence there, at the entrance to her body, and knew that only the thin fabric of her panties kept him from penetrating her.

Grant pulled back then, trembling slightly, his face dark, a vein prominent on his temple. His hair was still damp, and thoroughly rumpled, making him look dangerous, untamed, a far cry from the natty, refined Wall Street attorney the rest of the world knew.

He sat next to her. She tried to rise, but he pressed her back into the covers, perusing her from head to toe as if she were some luscious dessert and he was deciding whether to consume her slowly in little bitty bites or devour her all at once.

She said, "Grant, I...I think I'm ready."

He gave her a slow smile full of promise. "I'm glad to hear it. Now lie back and relax."

This is it, she thought, fully expecting him to just, well, do it. Instead he leaned casually on one palm and dragged his fingers up her arm and across her chest, so delicately that she shivered. He continued to stroke her, over the bustier and her bare midsection, with single-minded absorption.

Charli's skin tingled. Gradually she relaxed, even when the languid caress extended to her hips and legs, even when he parted her knees, just slightly, to brush his fingertips over the sensitive insides of her thighs. She hadn't thought she could be any more ready than she was, but the more Grant touched her, the harder it became to lie still. Her pulse quickened along with her breathing.

Now, Grant. I'm ready now. Really. She didn't say it, she just lay there, trying not to squirm too obviously.

"You have no idea how alluring you are." Grant captured her stiff nipple between his thumb and forefinger and lightly fondled it through the bustier. Charli's breath fled in a rush. "And it's not because of this getup you're wearing, although I must remember to thank Amanda for helping you choose it. It's you, Charli. You exude sensuality."

Charli couldn't help it. Her bark of laughter was instant and spontaneous.

Grant smiled. He released her nipple and let his hands roam once more. "Yours isn't the shallow, in-your-face brand of sensuality. Anyone can put on that kind of show. What you have goes deeper than that. It's...it's in the way you absentmindedly rub your fingers over the chenille pillow on the sofa when you're watching TV. Enjoying the texture, I suppose, but it always makes me fantasize about being that pillow. Or the way you taste something you're cooking. Your eyes kind of flutter shut, just for an instant. I'll bet you're not even aware of it."

She wasn't.

"Now that I got you into this thing—" he flipped her over "—let's see if it's just as much fun getting you out of it."

Charli lay on her stomach and let Grant work his way back down the interminable row of hooks and eyes. He released the last one and the material parted.

He tugged on the bustier and she obediently raised herself up a little so he could pull it away.

Abruptly freed from the constricting garment, she felt barer than bare. Grant moved her arms away from her sides. His palms left twin trails of heat as they glided down her back to the top of her panties, and up her sides to where her breasts were flattened against the bedspread. Charli was surprised to discover just how sensitive she was there. He continued the sensual massage, wringing a broken sigh from her.

Okay, Grant, now I'm really, really ready!

He turned her onto her back and leaned over to plant a hard, fast kiss on her softly panting mouth. "I know, sweetheart, I know," he whispered. "But bear with me a little longer. I've waited so long, I just can't get enough of you."

He proved it by kissing her throat and chest, lingering at her breasts, which he nibbled and suckled until she thought she might climax again, just from that. But Grant had other plans. Slowly he worked his way down her torso, leaving gooseflesh in his wake. His tongue flicked into her navel and she gasped.

Grant hooked his fingers over the top edge of her panties, easing them down her hips and legs. He parted her thighs and moved between them. Charli closed her eyes, light-headed with anticipation. *At last, oh yes, oh yes, oh—*

"Oh!" She jerked in alarm, automatically trying to push him away.

Grant smiled up from where he'd just kissed her, impervious to her efforts to dislodge him. "I told you, Charli, I can't get enough of you."

"We—we don't have to... I mean, it's too soon for this. Isn't it?"

"Since you're asking, no."

"Grant, I..." Charli knew couples sometimes loved each other in this way, and she couldn't deny the idea intrigued her, but she'd always thought of it as something exotic and forbidden, something jaded lovers did to keep sex exciting.

His smile was tender and devilish at once. "Trust me," he said again, and lowered his head. She felt his kiss as a hot buzz of pleasure, right there where she wept for him. It was followed by another, and yet another. Trembling, she collapsed back onto the bed.

"That's right," he murmured into her drenched flesh, "relax...give yourself up to it...."

And she did. He left her no choice. The surfeit of sensation was so great, she could only lie there and let it roll over her, like a tidal wave. His lips were voracious, his tongue strong and supple and unrelenting, giving her no respite from the breathtaking pleasure he was determined to give her. Charli's own hoarse cries rang in her ears. Her fingers threaded through the short, damp strands of Grant's hair, no longer trying to push him away but to hold him to her.

She was close to release when he reared over her and positioned himself. His eyes searched hers. "Hold on to me," he whispered, and she did, wrapping her arms around him, opening herself to him. The blunt pressure between her legs intensified as he slowly, carefully, began to press into her.

Charli failed to stifle a gasp of pain. Somehow, she

hadn't expected this piercing burn, the feeling of being invaded, stretched impossibly wide.

Grant placed a tender kiss on her lips. "It'll be better real soon, I promise. Try to relax—I won't rush."

True to his word, he held himself still, and after a few moments Charli managed to will the tension from her body. Somehow he sensed just the right instant to begin moving again, in short, measured thrusts. By the time he was fully within her, she was rising to meet him. She reached up to smooth the lines of tension from his brow.

His deep voice seemed to vibrate all through her. "Are you all right?"

Charli nodded, touched by his concern. "I love you," she whispered, her throat tight with emotion.

Grant didn't say the words she needed to hear, but he said it with his body, with the singular wonder of the act of love. They rocked together, in a slow, sweet cadence, as mounting pleasure eclipsed the initial pain. Many times she'd imagined what lovemaking must be like, but her imagination had fallen far short of reality. The sense of connectedness, of an inviolable bond, was as overwhelming as the astounding physical sensations.

Soon they both were coated with a sheen of sweat. Charli clamped her arms around Grant, and her legs, holding him close, the two of them locked in a frenzy of movement as the tension inside her coiled tighter and tighter. Just as she reached her peak, he uttered a strangled groan, driving into her hard and fast, forcing the very breath from her lungs. In that charmed instant, Charli had no doubt that she and Grant truly were one.

14

"I KNOW THAT PIECE." Eva Farman accepted a stick of batter-fried zucchini from one of the two hired servers circulating with platters of nibble food. "I'm no whiz when it comes to classical music, but it sounds familiar."

"It's the Pachelbel *Canon*," Grant said. "You don't have a drink. Can I get you another vodka tonic?"

Eva's gaze skittered around Grant's living room before alighting on her husband, Jim, over by the bay window. Jim wasn't looking their way; his attention was on the off-color joke Sam Kauffman was regaling him with.

"Oh, what the hell." Eva's conspiratorial whisper was slightly slurred as she grabbed Grant's arm and leaned into him just a little too closely. She seemed to be having difficulty keeping her balance. "I'd *love* another."

"You got it," he said, carefully easing out of her grasp and heading for the den, where a full bar had been set up. His uh-oh antenna was quivering. How many drinks had Eva consumed so far? Her furtive glances at her husband told Grant that her alcohol consumption was probably an issue between them.

Just what Grant needed. The wife of one of the firm's founding partners getting smashed and publicly embarrassing her husband. At Grant's home. Yes, that would do wonders for his bid for partner.

The large living room easily accommodated their ten guests, who'd been enjoying predinner cocktails and hors d'oeuvres for the past hour or so. As he made his way to the den, Grant spotted Charli chatting animatedly with Eileen Van Cleave and Sarah Holm, the wives of the two other founding partners. The tension in his shoulders cranked up a notch. What were they talking about? What kind of impression was Charli making?

As he passed them he heard her say with a laugh, "...burnt to cinders! The smoke alarm was screaming, and Grant and I were running around like maniacs, tossing charred bruschetta into the sink—"

"My bride has the gift of exaggeration," Grant interrupted, hoping his smile didn't look as forced as it felt. "To her, a few pieces of overdone garlic bread constitute a major conflagration. It was no big deal. A little concentration on her part and it wouldn't even have happened."

Eileen and Sarah tittered. Charli's smile was strained. He hadn't meant to embarrass her, but what was she thinking, turning that disaster into a topic of conversation? The truth was, she *had* let the bruschetta burn to cinders. She'd turned her back on the oven for a few moments to prepare the batter for the zucchini, and one of their appetizers had gone up in smoke.

Grant excused himself to fetch Eva's drink. He might have let one of the rent-a-maids get it, if he weren't intent on making it weak enough to keep Eva from making a drunken fool of herself. He could have used a couple of shots himself tonight, to help relieve the strain, but he didn't dare. He had to be "on" with this crowd, sharp and alert, and that meant tossing back ginger ales in the guise of Scotch and soda.

He dropped ice into a glass and added an eyedropper worth of vodka. As he was topping it off with tonic water, he heard someone else enter the den, and glanced up to see Charli. She looked incredible in that short, navy silk dress. It's off-the-shoulder styling and formfitting cut were mercilessly distracting. Her hair fell softly around her face, flowing over her silky bare shoulders. He couldn't look at her without thinking about what they'd done that afternoon, in her room.

Logically, he knew it had been a mistake. The rational part of him wished it had never happened. What were they supposed to do now? They couldn't turn back the clock. Now that he'd had her, he knew without a doubt he'd have her again; he wasn't capable of living under the same roof with a woman as bewitching as his wife and keeping his hands off her.

If they could manage to keep it on the level of pure sexual gratification, they could probably make it work. But it was already too late for that. The passion and tenderness Grant had felt while making love to Charli had overwhelmed him. During the past weeks he'd fantasized about being her first, and by God, he had been! It had been extraordinary, eclipsing his fantasies. The immense physical pleasure had been only part of it. He'd been unprepared for the beauty and wonder of making love with his own wife.

His wife. His sensual, alluring bride, who'd saved

herself for her husband, for the one true love of her life. Who'd saved herself for him.

No, he hadn't expected that devastating emotional connection; even now, hours later, he struggled to shake off the poignant afterglow, to refocus on his goals. He shoved the question of what the hell to do about his marriage to a back burner, and forced himself to concentrate on the purpose of this dinner party—positioning himself as prime partner material, complete with a stable home life and the ideal "team player" wife.

With every minute that passed, Grant's nervous agitation increased. This evening was critical to his career. He needed every detail to be perfect, and the unforeseen snafus—like Charli ruining the bruschetta and blabbing about it—were making him crazy. And they hadn't yet served the first course!

He kept his eyes on his task as he capped the bottle of tonic and perched a wedge of lemon on Eva's drink. "You didn't buy any horseradish for bloody Marys, Charli. I put it on the list. Along with cocktail onions for Frank's martinis, which you also forgot."

"I can live without onions."

Frank's voice was like a belt to the solar plexus, jerking Grant's head around. He hadn't noticed Frank entering right behind Charli.

"If you have olives, that'll be fine." Frank ambled to the bar.

"Oh, I'll fix it for you," Charli said, scooting past Grant, her movements a little stiff. He could tell she didn't take kindly to being criticized in front of Frank.

Well, hell, Grant wouldn't have said it if he'd known they weren't alone.

"Gin or vodka?" Charli produced a martini glass and shaker.

"Vodka," Frank said. "And dry as a bone—just wave the bottle of vermouth over it."

Charli lifted the small crystal bowl of green olives. It slipped from her fingers and shattered on the parquet floor.

"Charli!" Grant scooted out of the line of fire as glass shards and olives sprayed in all directions. "Great. That's great. Don't tell me—that was the last of the olives."

"I'll—I'll get a broom."

"No," he practically growled. She'd do it, too—start sweeping up the mess herself, right in front of everyone. "That's what we hired people for, Charli."

"I'll go find one of them," Frank said, on his way out the door.

Charli glanced around to ensure their privacy, and hissed, "Why are you doing this?"

"Doing what? Trying to have a successful party?"

"Grant, for heaven's sake, it's not the end of the world if there are no cocktail onions. Or—or—" She gestured at the mess on the floor. "You've got me so rattled, I don't know what I'm doing."

"Oh, so it's my fault you dropped it?"

She pressed her fingers to her temples, shook her head. "Just try to calm down, okay? Little glitches always crop up when you're entertaining. It happens."

From the living room came the buzz of chatter, a burst of laughter. Grant stepped close to Charli. He got right in her face, his voice low and rough. "This isn't just any party, Charli. This isn't Nonni's birthday party at the Knights of Columbus hall. This is business. *Everything* matters. The goddamn onions matter if it's Frank Van Cleave who wants them. That's what all this is about. Business." He gestured widely, encompassing her, him, the house, their guests. "It's what *all* of it is about. I don't know how to make it any clearer."

She stared at him, motionless. Her eyes were wide and moist, her color high. Her throat worked for a moment. Finally she whispered, "No, you've made it clear enough."

"Damn it, Charli, this is not news to you. Don't do this. Just because we slept together doesn't mean my priorities have changed."

"Of course not." Her chin jerked up. "I'll try not to do anything too gauche for the rest of the evening."

"Charli—"

One of the rent-a-maids bustled in with a broom and a roll of paper towels. Eva Farman appeared in the doorway. "Did you forget about me, Grant? Oh. What happened here?"

"Nothing, just a minor spill." He handed Eva her weak drink. It wouldn't hurt to get something in her stomach to soak up the booze. "Have you tried the stuffed mushrooms?"

After Charli's revelation to Sarah and Eileen about the burned bruschetta, Grant kept a tight rein on her conversations with the partners and their wives. On several occasions he nipped a questionable topic in the bud, studiously ignoring the speaking looks Charli leveled at him, easily deciphered as *mind your own business.*

This is *my business!* he wanted to remind her, as his blood pressure ratcheted up another notch.

Charli finally got Frank's martini made, only to toss it right in his face. To be fair, it wasn't her fault. Eva threw her arms wide in describing her new cabin cruiser, knocking Charli off balance just as she was handing the glass to Frank.

Frank Van Cleave, drenched in vodka! Frank laughed off this latest martini-related mishap—"Something tells me I should stick to beer"—but by this time, Grant was one giant, throbbing tension headache. He responded with a pithy gibe at his wife's clumsiness, a knee-jerk attempt to defuse the situation. He could tell he'd hurt Charli's feelings, but he couldn't let Eva take the blame. The last thing he wanted was to draw attention to Eva's state of inebriation—although if her husband's narrow-eyed gaze was any indication, he was beginning to get the picture.

Dinner was superb, of course, although Grant had to force down every bite, his stomach was so tied in knots from stress. He felt compelled to offer an apologetic comment about the stew, served as the second course after risotto with asparagus. Not that the *spezzatino di vitello alla salvia* wasn't absolutely delicious, and elegantly presented, but it was, after all, stew, and Grant couldn't help but feel self-conscious about presenting it to this chateaubriand crowd. His guests laughed off his concern as they gorged themselves on the savory tidbits of tender veal delicately flavored with sage and white wine. Charli's expression remained neutral, even as embarrassed color flooded her face. She avoided eye contact with him for the duration of the meal.

The third course was a Jerusalem artichoke and spinach salad, followed by a combined cheese and fruit course. By the time they retired to the living room for coffee, the replete guests all claimed they had no room for dessert. Nevertheless, when Charli unveiled her luscious *gelato di caffè con la cioccolata calda*—homemade espresso ice cream with hot chocolate sauce—no one had the will to resist.

Their guests lingered for several more hours, enjoying strong Italian coffee and animated conversation. Grant took it as a good sign that no one seemed in a hurry to leave. Eventually, however, the party wound down. Frank and Eileen Van Cleave were the last to depart, just before two in the morning, effusive in their praise and demanding recipes and an invitation to the next get-together.

Grant and Charli helped the rent-a-maids clean up. He tipped them generously and saw them off, as Charli disappeared upstairs. He turned off the lights, set the house alarm and climbed the stairs, snagging a couple of antacids from the bathroom and munching them as he passed the closed door of her bedroom.

"I think it went well," he called to her.

No answer. Could she be asleep already? In his own room, Grant pulled off his clothes and slipped on his black silk robe, mechanically tying it at the waist as he wandered back to Charli's room. Now that the strain of the party was behind him, he felt lighthearted, buoyant. He wanted to talk over the evening with Charli, compare notes.

But that wasn't all he wanted. Was she still wearing that sexy cocktail dress? He hoped so. He'd enjoy getting her out of it, and out of that outrageous bustier yet again.

He knocked lightly on her door. "Charli?"

Silence.

"You're not asleep, are you? Sweetheart?" Knock knock.

When she still didn't respond, he carefully eased the door open, expecting to see her tucked under the covers in her darkened bedroom. A smile of anticipation stretched his face. He'd wake her gently, and love her until the sun came up.

To his surprise, the room was well lit. Grant's gaze zeroed in on Charli's bed, and the half-filled suitcase lying open on it.

15

CHARLI GLANCED at her husband, standing in the open doorway of her room, as she tossed a pile of underwear in her suitcase and went back to the dresser for more clothes.

Grant came into the room, frowning at the suitcase. His frown deepened as he took in her attire, slacks and a short-sleeved cotton sweater. "What's going on, Charli? What's this about?"

"I'm leaving."

His eyes widened in shock and confusion. He shook his head, as if what he was witnessing defied belief.

Charli pulled a couple of dresses out of her closet at random and crammed them into the suitcase. "I'll send my brother Robby for the rest of my stuff."

Grant reached her in two long strides and seized her shoulders. "What the hell has gotten into you?"

She shook him off and crossed to the dresser, snatching up hairbrushes and her old jewelry box. The jewelry Grant had given her lay on the dresser top; she left it there. "It's called cutting my losses."

"Cutting your losses?" He threw his arms wide. "You're talking about our marriage, not some poker game! Talk to me, Charli. You're not going anywhere till you tell me—"

"I'll go wherever I damn well please," she said, facing him directly, her voice low and determined. "I'm sorry if that doesn't sound very 'accommodating,' or 'undemanding,' but deal with it."

He took a slow, deep breath. She sensed him reining in his tongue, groping for the right words. "Whatever prompted this, let's...sleep on it. Talk it over in the morning."

"Sorry." She slammed the top of the bulging suitcase, ruthlessly stuffing garments into it, finally managing to latch it. "I'm not spending one more night sequestered in this lonely little bedroom."

"Is that what this is about? After this afternoon... Charli, you don't have to sleep alone tonight. I'll stay with you."

"Oh, thank you!" She gestured broadly, dripping sarcasm. "My husband deigns to share my bed. *I'm so goddamn grateful!*"

He gaped at her, clearly taken aback by the depth of her anger. "Why now?" he asked. "Why tonight? After our party, which was so successful?"

"*Your* party."

He said nothing.

"I'm surprised to hear you describe it as successful."

"Why?" he asked. "You saw how late everyone stayed, how much they enjoyed the food, the company, everything."

"Then why did you spend the entire evening trying to embarrass me?"

"I— Charli, why do you say that? I wasn't trying to—"

"No? Then I guess it just comes naturally to you. Either way, it was inexcusable." Somehow, she'd managed to comport herself with dignity and grace until the last guest had walked out the door.

"What?" he said. "Is it that remark I made when you spilled the drink on Frank?"

"It wasn't just that one instance. You know what I'm talking about. You turned me into some kind of whipping girl for every minor snafu that occurred, someone to blame and ridicule at every turn."

"Come on. I didn't ridicule you."

He said it without conviction. Charli just stared at him, until his gaze slid away.

"Okay, maybe I was a little... I could've been more..." He sighed. "I was under a lot of pressure."

"And I wasn't?"

"It wasn't the same for you."

"Because it was all about you, about business."

He opened his mouth—to object, she could tell—then seemed to think better of it. Perhaps he remembered their earlier conversation during the party.

"That *is* what you said, isn't it?" she persisted. "That it's all about business—the party, our marriage, everything."

Last week he'd said something different. *My making partner isn't the sole purpose of our marriage. Not anymore.* She'd believed him then, because she'd wanted to. Perhaps he'd wanted to believe it as well; perhaps on some level he, too, was uncomfortable with their cold-blooded "arrangement." But his words tonight, and his actions, revealed his true feelings, to both of them.

"If your party was a success," she said, "it's because

I bent over backward to make it one. All for the sake of my husband and his precious career!''

"Look." He thrust his hands into the pockets of his robe. "I mishandled some things tonight. I admit it."

His complacent expression told Charli he considered this lukewarm apology sufficient. She hauled the suitcase off the bed onto the floor. He watched it land with a thud. "It was nerves, okay?" he said. "No big deal."

She grabbed her purse, hefted the suitcase and headed for the door, shoving him away as he reached for the handle of the suitcase—not to help carry it, she knew, but to keep her from leaving.

Grant followed her down the hall. "Charli, I said some stupid things. I hurt your feelings— I didn't mean to. It was a one-time thing. It won't happen again."

He stood at the top of the steps and watched her wrestle the heavy suitcase to the front door. "Damn it, Charli! I never thought you'd run away because of some stupid little thing like this."

Dropping the bag in the entry foyer, she swung around to face him. "That's not the whole reason and you know it. This afternoon meant nothing to you, Grant. What we shared."

"That's not true."

"You said it yourself!" she accused. "That just because we slept together didn't mean anything had changed. You said that."

"That's not...I never said it didn't mean anything to me." Slowly he descended the stairs. "I only meant it didn't change the kind of arrange—"

"Don't call it that!" she cried. "It's not an arrangement, Grant, it's a marriage. A *marriage!* We spoke vows!" Charli pulled her wedding and engagement rings off her finger and set them on the console table with a trembling hand.

Grant stopped halfway down the staircase. His troubled gaze went from the rings to her face.

Charli's voice shook. "You know, it actually occurred to me, during the party, that maybe...maybe you made love to me out of pity."

"Charli..."

"But I know, deep down, it wasn't that. At one time I would've thought so, but no longer. I know you care for me, Grant, though you can't admit it—to either of us. And maybe our lovemaking did mean something to you. I thought so at the time, but that could've been just more wishful thinking."

"Don't run off," he said quietly, coming the rest of the way down the stairs. "You're tired, I'm tired. Tomorrow we'll be fresher, and we'll be able to—"

"No we won't. We can't fix this, because you were right. Nothing has changed. This marriage is still about you, and it always will be. I thought, when we made love...I thought it meant that you value me as highly as you do your career. I was wrong."

Charli hadn't known her husband could look this pained. His eyes closed briefly, but he said nothing. They stood a few feet apart in the entry foyer, neither making a move to close the distance between them.

With an effort, she lifted her chin. "I deserve better. I deserve a husband who values me, who appreciates me—who loves me. And I deserve children. *Molto bambini!*"

Charli stabbed buttons on the house alarm keypad to deactivate it, lifted her suitcase and swung open the door. A damp night breeze wafted in.

She turned to face her husband one last time. "You're a matrimonial lawyer. I don't want anything from you. Just send the divorce papers. I'll sign them and we'll be rid of each other. Goodbye, Grant."

16

"MR. STERLING, there's a Ms. Rossi on line two."

Something thumped hard inside Grant's chest. He leaned back in his leather office chair and dragged in a deep, calming breath.

Charli.

"I'll take the call, Sandy."

It had been over three weeks since she'd left him, three hellish weeks spent waiting for the phone to ring, for her to show up on his doorstep. He'd known she'd come back to him, but he hadn't expected it to take nearly this long.

Somewhere along the line, his shy, tractable wife had changed. And so had he. He found he liked her with backbone and a healthy measure of self-respect. Of course, it wreaked havoc on his original vision of a dry, practical marriage, but somehow, that particular vision had lost its allure.

The prospect of spending the rest of his life without Charli had done a number on his priorities. If it took a little compromise to get her back, so be it. And since she was the one initiating contact, his lawyerly side reasoned, perhaps he wouldn't have to compromise all that much. Her making the first move put him in a position of strength. He was glad now that he hadn't given in to the often overwhelming urge to jump in the car, drive over to her parents' place and beg her to return.

Grant took another deep breath as he pushed the button to connect to his caller. He forced a casual tone. "Charli. How have you been?"

There was a moment's pause, then a voice said, "Grant, this is Maria Rossi."

His fingers clenched around the receiver. Who? It was a woman's voice, but deeper, a little older sounding than Charli's.

"Charli's cousin," she explained. "I have a law practice out here in Great Neck. I believe you were instructed to send me the separation agreement?"

A vise clamped around Grant's chest. Maria Rossi, Esquire. Charli's brother Robby had given him her card when he'd picked up Charli's belongings the day after she'd left. Grant was expected to draw up the separation agreement and send it to Maria for a legal look-see before Charli signed it. The first step to a quick, painless divorce.

"Are you there?" Maria asked.

"I'm here."

"Grant, I'm still waiting for that agreement. Charli's getting a little impatient. She wants this wrapped up as soon as possible."

"I've...been busy," he said.

"I can draft it here. I'll have it in your hands by the end of the week. All you have to do is look it over and sign it."

"No. I'll get to it." Grant rubbed the back of his neck. "I'll, uh, make it a priority."

He detected a touch of irritation in Maria's tone

when she said, "Look, we'll probably save time if I just get the ball rolling from this end. We're not talking any tricky negotiations here. Charli doesn't want a penny from you—against the advice of counsel, I might add—but she's determined to streamline this, and it's my job to help her do that. So what's it going to be?"

He pulled in a ragged breath, and let it out. "I'll work on it today."

"If I don't receive the agreement from you by Friday, I'll generate it from here," she said crisply. "You have my address?"

"Um...I think I may have misplaced your card." He'd misplaced it in his kitchen garbage can, in about a dozen little pieces, as soon as Robby had left.

Maria recited her firm's address. He jotted it down on a yellow legal pad and sat looking at it for several minutes after he hung up the phone.

She really wants out. The cold, unyielding truth of it settled over him like frost.

Grant leaned his elbows on his desk, his chin propped on the knuckles of his linked hands. He ignored the intercom buzzer, ignored the stack of work awaiting his attention. Finally he tore the top sheet off the legal pad and ripped up Maria Rossi's address for the second time. He strode to the door, snatching his suit jacket off a chair on the way. As he passed his secretary's desk he said, "Cancel my appointments for the rest of the day, Sandy. An emergency's come up."

"You like my *bocconcini fritti*, eh?" Grandma Rossi gingerly eased her bulk onto the picnic-table bench next to Grant. He leaped up and offered his assistance as she settled herself with a small grunt of exertion.

"It's delicious, Nonni." She'd produced a platter of assorted fried tidbits while Charli's brother Eddie mounded charcoal in the barbecue grill, emptied most of a can of lighter fluid into it and sacrificed the hair on the back of his hand by tossing in a lit match.

Nonni pushed the platter closer to Grant. She pointed to a breaded chunk. "You tried the mortadella and cheese?"

"It's my favorite. I've got to slow down, though, or I won't have room for anything else." For the dozenth time he glanced behind him to the side gate of Joe and Betty Rossi's backyard.

"She'll be here." Nonni patted Grant's hand. "It's her papa's birthday."

Grant had tried calling Charli from the road, only to have her mother inform him that she wasn't living at her parents' house. She'd found a one-bedroom apartment near Courtland High School. For the first time in her life, Charli had her own place.

But she'd be coming over today, Betty had added, in the late afternoon right after work, for a barbecue party in honor of Joe's seventy-fifth birthday. Grant's mother-in-law had been quick to issue him an invitation. He knew that the Rossis had to be distressed by their youngest daughter's separation from her husband. They were conservative, religious people with traditional values. He didn't know what Charli had told them, but he suspected she hadn't run him down too much. Not only was she not the vindictive type, but Betty and Joe had welcomed him warmly today. Obviously they were hoping for a reconciliation.

It was a hot, hazy day in mid-June. Grant had left his jacket and necktie in the car. Now he rolled up the sleeves of his white dress shirt. A bottle of Pete's Wicked Ale materialized in front of him.

"I'll enjoy it vicariously through you," Charli's sister Angie said as she sat down opposite him. She was about seven months pregnant and had to shove the bench back to make room for her belly. Her gaze fixed on a point behind Grant. She gave a little wave. Grant's heart skipped a few beats. He took a deep draft of his beer.

"I would've been here sooner," he heard Charli call, "but I had to go home to—"

She stopped abruptly, and he knew she'd spotted him. He turned in his seat. She stood on the lawn about twenty feet away, holding a huge glass bowl covered with plastic wrap. Her stony expression did not inspire hope.

Charli turned to her mother, bustling out of the back door with a pan full of raw, marinated chicken pieces. "You shouldn't have asked him here, Mama. It's not right to interfere."

"*He* called *us!*" Betty screeched, giving her daughter a wide berth as she scurried to the grill. "Are the coals ready yet? No? Eddie, put more lighter fluid on it."

Charli's father bestirred himself from the lawn chair where he'd been nursing a beer. "You'll put out the fire if you add more fluid! Leave it alone! It'll get hot!"

"When?" Betty cried. "Everyone's hungry!"

Charli hadn't moved. Grant rose and approached her. He peeked through the plastic wrap to see what she'd brought: a colorful pasta salad laden with small chunks of salami, cheese and vegetables.

"Looks good."

"You shouldn't have come here, Grant."

"Let me help you with this." He took the bowl from her and brought it to the picnic table. When he returned to Charli, her expression hadn't softened. He got the feeling she was deciding whether to stay or leave.

"Why are you doing this?" she asked.

He kept his voice low, mindful of all the eager ears nearby. "Charli, I'm not trying to cause trouble, I don't want to disrupt your father's birthday, I just want to talk to you."

"We talked. I've been waiting three weeks for that separation agreement."

"I know. Let's go inside, find a quiet place to discuss this."

God, how he'd missed her. He stared at her, drinking in every detail. She'd kept her new hairstyle, soft and wispy around her face, the rest pulled back in a low ponytail. She'd paired a snug, sleeveless, fire-engine red T-shirt with a black denim skirt that fell to a few inches above her knees. Her legs were bare and ended in strappy, black patent sandals. It was a flattering, youthful outfit, one she'd never have considered wearing just two months earlier.

"There's no point to this, Grant. Please. This whole thing, the divorce, could go so much more smoothly if we just—"

"I don't want it to go smoothly. I just want it to go away." The backyard chatter had died down; Grant felt several pairs of eyes burning into his back. "Now, we can find someplace private or we can discuss this here, in front of your family. But I have a few things to say, and I'm not leaving till I say them."

Charli responded with a flat, hard stare. Two months ago she would have been cowed, would have done anything to avoid a scene. Two months ago she probably would have seen this whole mess as her own fault.

"Okay." He raised his palms. "I know how over-bearing that sounded. It's just that...I'm losing you and it's my own damn fault and I don't know how to stop it."

"You're afraid a divorce will tarnish your chances of making partner."

"No. That's not—"

"Just blame it on me. Tell them you found out I'm, I don't know, a drug addict or a bigamist or— I don't care what you say about me, Grant. I hope you make partner, I really do. But I'm not interested in being your PR manager. I already have a job. What I could use is a husband."

"You have one." Before she could object, he added, "I'll quit the firm."

Whatever Charli had been about to say died on her tongue. She blinked at him, mute. Finally her gaze flicked around the busy backyard. Grudgingly she said, "Come on," and led him inside the house.

Grant followed her up the stairs and into a small, stuffy bedroom with a sloping ceiling and faded floral wallpaper. The narrow twin bed was neatly made, covered with a pink chenille bedspread. An antique mirror hung over the small dressing table. The dark oak flooring was partially concealed by an oval braided rug.

"This was your room?" Grant asked.

Charli nodded. She closed the door for privacy and raised the gingham-draped window, which looked out on the backyard. A desultory breeze carried the scent of smoldering charcoal and the muted sounds of conversation. "I shared it with Donna and Angie until they got married. There was a bunk bed over there." She pointed to the wall opposite the bed, now occupied by three mismatched bookcases crammed with paperbacks.

Grant sat on the bed. It was too soft; the springs protested his weight. He'd hoped Charli would sit next to him, but instead she turned the dressing-table chair around and parked herself there.

"I don't believe you," she said. "I don't believe you'd quit the firm."

"I could go back to the D.A.'s office. It was satisfying work, putting away the bad guys. The money's not so great, but with my savings, and your income, we should be able to keep the house."

Her gaze sharpened at his mention of her income. When they'd first married, she'd wanted to merge their money, to contribute financially to the marriage. He'd dismissed the idea out of hand. Only during the past three weeks of soul-searching had he realized how offended he would have been if the roles had been reversed and his life partner had acted as if the fruit of his labors meant nothing.

"Or I could hang out a shingle," Grant said. "Start my own practice. I have to admit, the idea's always intrigued me. Of course, if I did that, we'd be even more strapped for cash. Especially in the beginning."

She looked skeptical. "What about your goal? The partnership?"

Grant struggled for the words to express what he felt. She had to see it in his face, his eyes. When he spoke at last, his voice was choked with honest emotion. "Charli, sweetheart…I would do anything, give up anything, to keep you."

She shook her head, uncomprehending. "Grant, it's the driving force of your life, the need to make partner. It means more to you than anything."

"Not anymore. It *used to* mean more to me than anything, back when I thought I knew what I needed to make me happy, to complete my life. You give me—" he spread his hands "—what I never knew I needed. A partnership would be nice, I wouldn't turn it down, but I could live without it. I could get used to a different job, less income, a simpler way of life. I could never get used to not having you in my life."

Charli wrapped her arms around herself; she dropped her gaze to her lap. "You'd always resent me—if you gave up your dream on account of me." In a small voice she added, "I couldn't live with that, Grant. Seeing it in your eyes, day after day. Don't tell me you wouldn't be bitter." She lifted her stricken face to his. "But I couldn't go back to the way it was for us, either."

"It'll never be that way again, I swear it, whether or not I stay at the firm." He paused, steeling himself. "I know it's always frustrated you that I wouldn't talk about my past. My childhood, my family. And I know I don't have any right to ask it of you now, after...after everything, but I want to tell you about it, if you'll listen. I've never told anyone. Well, except for Raven, in our hypnotherapy sessions, but even she hasn't heard all of it." Grant's voice was tight; his palms sweated.

Charli whispered, "Why now?"

"I need you to know *me*, the real me...." He swallowed hard. "I need you to know what brought me to this point, before you decide to walk away."

She gave a little nod, her expression sober.

Grant took a deep breath. "I'm an only child. I grew up in a small town in rural Pennsylvania. We didn't have much money. It was..." He shook his head. How to describe that which he had yet to come to terms with? How to make Charli understand? "My parents had a volatile marriage. I can't remember one single day when things were calm at home."

"They fought a lot?"

"They fought, yes, and it usually got physical. But the next minute they'd be sobbing out their undying love, begging each other not to leave. Every fight ended up in bed, it seemed. Their marriage was the ultimate love-hate relationship."

"And you were caught in the middle."

"I never wanted to come home from school. I stayed after whenever I could, doing my homework in the school library, asking for extra assignments. Just so I could delay going home." He smiled wryly. "On the plus side, my grades were terrific."

"Grant...those scars on your back."

"Dad slapped Mom around, but he never did any real damage to her. Maybe he was afraid she really would leave him if he did. So he took most of his rage out on me. Especially when I got a little older, eleven or twelve. I started standing up to him then, and I guess he saw that as a threat."

Charli's features tightened in pain. "What did he do to you?"

"Dad was a construction worker. He had a lot of stuff he'd pilfered off various jobs, including this length of steel cable."

"Oh, God..."

Grant could still picture that thick piece of cable, about eighteen inches long with exposed strands of steel at its frayed ends. "He started taking that thing to my back on a regular basis. Dad was big, a bruiser. He'd lay into me with that cable, tearing up my back, and the worst of it was...Mom did nothing to stop him."

"Could she have?"

"I don't know. She could've tried. I didn't want the old man to see me cry, and I fought the tears as long as I could. But he refused to stop until he'd broken me down. Then he'd sneer and call me a wimp and tell me I'd never be the man he was."

"I should hope to God not." Charli shuddered. "How long did it go on?"

"Until I ran away at sixteen."

"Where did you go?"

"To Philadelphia first. I lived on the streets. I'd heard I had relatives on Long Island, so eventually I made my way here, hitchhiking. But my cousins didn't want anything to do with me—they just threatened to send for my old man—so I ended up fending for myself, taking whatever odd jobs I could get, crashing anywhere someone was willing to lend me a little floor space."

Leaning forward, he rested his elbows on his thighs, letting his hands dangle between his knees. He studied the pattern on the worn braided rug as he said, "I lived for a while with this girl. A few years older than me. She worked checkout at a supermarket where I bagged groceries. I wasn't in love with her or anything, but it was a real bed for the first time in months, so I let her think I was."

He glanced up at Charli. If she was repelled by these revelations, she gave no clue.

"At some point," she said, "you must've gone back to school."

"Eventually I was able to finish high school. I kept working while I was attending Queens College, and later, NYU Law School. I was a good student, so I got a couple of scholarships, but mostly I got by with student loans. Passed the bar on my first try and accepted a position with the Manhattan district attorney's office."

Charli was studying him intently. "I can't imagine the perseverance that must've taken. The sheer grit and belief in yourself. To go from, well, from an abused child to where you are now, all by yourself with no one else's help."

"I made a promise to myself, Charli. Shortly after I ran away from home, when I was living on the streets. I vowed to get as far from my past as possible. Nowadays they call it 'reinventing yourself.' I called it survival. My ultimate goal was the affluence and respectability I could never have achieved back home." He didn't state the obvious, that that was where a partnership in Farman, Van Cleave and Holm came in.

She asked, "Did you ever go back to see your parents?"

He shook his head. "They never looked for me, either, as far as I can tell. They could've found me easily enough, through my social security number. I never changed my name or tried to hide."

Charli's expression told him she had trouble understanding how parents could be so irreparably estranged from their son. She'd grown up in a big, loving family. The Rossis weren't much better off, financially, than his family had been, but they were immeasurably richer in so many ways.

"I understand now," Charli said slowly. "I understand why you were so intent on attaining the goal you set for yourself. Thank you for sharing this with me."

He drew in an unsteady breath. "You're my wife. I should never have kept it from you."

Moisture sprang to her eyes; she blinked it away. "Our marriage was different. It wasn't expected that we'd share ourselves that way."

"*I* didn't expect it, you mean." He searched her face, willing her to recognize the depth of his sincerity. "I love you, Charli."

Her eyes squeezed shut and a tear rolled down her cheek.

"I want ours to be a real marriage," he continued, "the kind with sex and kids and disagreements and the fun of making up afterward. And fidelity—I can't imagine ever wanting another woman. What I feel for you...sweetheart, it's so right. So special. Our marriage could never descend into the kind of twisted relationship my folks had. I know that now."

Grant rose. He walked over to Charli and pulled her off the chair and into his arms. "You were right when you said you deserve better. But if you're willing to give me another chance, I promise I won't disappoint you. I need you, Charli. I love you to distraction. I only hope it's not too late to start over."

He kissed her, a deep, feverish mating of mouths. She clung to him, pressed her body close, as fresh tears spilled. She tasted of salt and the wonder of new beginnings.

"Marry me," he murmured. "A real wedding this time, in a church in front of God and everyone we know. A fresh start. Say yes."

Charli pulled back, breathless, her dark eyes shining. "You don't have to quit the firm—not to prove something to me. Why don't we wait and see if you make partner this year?"

"Whatever. Marry me.'"

"I love you, Grant."

"Say yes, sweetheart. Marry me again."

"Yes. Yes, I'll marry you."

He stumbled backward and fell with her onto the bed, to the squealing accompaniment of rusty springs.

The mattress bounced a few times before sagging in the middle, wedging them together, maddening Grant with the intimate press of Charli's body as the two of them yanked at clothing, struggled with buttons and zippers.

They were naked within seconds, slippery with sweat in the sultry little room under the eaves. They writhed in a tangle on the small bed, touching and stroking and rediscovering each other. Charli was flushed with arousal, her nipples tightly pebbled, her lips dark and swollen from his kisses.

"I love you," Grant whispered as he rolled her beneath him on the swaybacked mattress. "Let's make a baby." Her body opened to him, stretched slick and tight around him as he pressed slowly into her. Charli tensed, but only for a moment, then she was moving with him, lifting to meet him, their mingled sweat a lubricant between their surging bodies.

The bed springs squeaked in time to their frenzied movements, louder, faster, until they stopped, shaking with muffled laughter, certain the racket carried through the open window into the backyard. Grant heaved himself off the bed, landing on his back on the braided rug with Charli sprawled on top of him. He guided her hips, and within moments they'd found their rhythm once more.

Charli's hair was a wild, dark mass, tickling his chest as she rode him. Her mouth was parted, panting, prompting Grant to reach up and stroke her lip, to slide his finger into her mouth and touch her tongue. She sucked his finger and he groaned deep in his throat, feeling himself grow even harder, if that was possible.

Her breasts swayed provocatively with her movements, drawing his hands. He cupped the heavy, satiny flesh, teased the stiff tips. She responded with sharp little sighs of pleasure, which turned into one long, feral whimper as her eyes fluttered shut and her hips hitched hard and fast against him. Her sweet, shuddering climax cascaded over him, through him, inviting him to spill himself in a blinding torrent of sensation.

Charli collapsed on Grant in a boneless heap. He stroked her back, her bottom, their galloping hearts pressed close together. Outside, the sounds of conversation had increased; more relatives must have arrived. The aromas of grilled chicken and hot dogs filled the small room.

Charli leaned up groggily. She smiled down at him. He reached up to flick away a damp tendril of hair stuck to her eyelid. She said, "I guess it's Sunny's turn now."

"Uh...if you say so. Just give me a few minutes to recover."

She smacked him playfully on the shoulder. "As if I'd share you! I like Sunny, but not *that* much."

"It's her turn for what?"

Charli gave him a beatific smile. "Let me tell you about the Wedding Ring."

Epilogue

THE TUXEDO-CLAD EMCEE brought the mike to his mouth. "At this time I'm going to ask all the single ladies to come out on the dance floor!"

He didn't have to ask twice. Sunny Bleecker was out of her seat like a shot, jockeying for position among the throng of unmarried women congregating on the dance floor. She watched Charli find her spot some distance in front of them, clutching her ball-shaped bouquet of cream and pink roses.

Charli was a picture-perfect bride in her exquisite, white satin gown. The fitted, sleeveless bodice, with its squared-off scoop neckline, was enhanced with delicate white satin floral appliqués. Columns of seed pearls had been sewn into an hourglass pattern of tucks on the front of the bodice, which ended in a V above the unadorned full skirt. Charli's hair was pulled back into a chignon surrounded by a circlet of cream rosebuds. During the ceremony a long, sheer veil edged in white satin had hung from the circlet.

Charli looked jubilant, and very much in love. Her bridegroom—and husband of two and a half months—stood on the fringes of the crowd, wearing a look of such besotted devotion that Sunny just knew their marriage would be a long and lively one. It had been a double-ring ceremony, at Grant's insistence. His wedding band, a barrel of plain brushed platinum, looked dramatic against his long, suntanned fingers.

Now it was Sunny's turn for happily ever after, and she was determined to give herself every edge. Charli presented her back, preparing to toss the bouquet over her shoulder toward her single female friends and relatives, some of whom were making disdainful noises about not even wanting to get married.

Then get your butt out of here and make room for those of us who do! Sunny wanted to shout. Catching the bridal bouquet might be baseless superstition, but at this point she was willing to try anything.

The band played some sort of bouquet-tossing music, complete with a drumroll, and Charli pitched the thing over her shoulder, putting a little spin on it. Sunny lifted the hem of her vintage chiffon dress and barreled through the crowd of women like an NFL linebacker, never taking her eyes off the bouquet. She tracked its progress as it arced up and to the right, making note of its speed and probable point of touchdown.

In the corner of her vision she spied one of Charli's Detroit cousins, the tall one in the hot pink tube dress, moving in for the kill. Fortunately, the cousin was hampered by three-inch heels. Ha! Sunny had slipped off her shoes at the table!

As the floral arrangement entered its final approach, Sunny watched the cousin easily reach over the heads of her neighbors, her heavily mascaraed eyes sparking with triumph. Sunny took a flying leap and cut off the cousin in midcatch, knocking her back and snagging the prize!

Sunny belted out a howl of triumph, holding the bouquet aloft while the cousin made some sneering comment to her pals and yanked up the top of that sausage casing she called a dress.

"I didn't even try," Amanda said, coming up beside Sunny. "I wasn't willing to risk getting a few teeth knocked out."

"You didn't try because you don't want to be the next to get married," Sunny said, breathing hard, swiping a long strand of auburn hair off her cheek. Amanda had never even set down her glass of champagne! "I wouldn't mind tossing my own bouquet—the sooner, the better."

Amanda shrugged. "Be my guest. I only hope you find marital bliss a more blissful experience than I did."

Charli and Raven joined them, offering congratulations and teasing Sunny about her cutthroat tactics.

"I've never seen so many women trying to catch the bouquet," Amanda said. "Although I shouldn't be surprised—there must be three hundred people here."

"Three hundred twenty," Charli said. "Our first wedding, back in April, was, well, you know it was a private civil ceremony at home. This time Grant insisted on a huge church wedding—and this lavish reception. Not that I'm complaining. This is the kind of wedding I've always dreamed of. I still can't believe we pulled it off with only a few weeks notice. And the best part is—" she glanced around to check who was within earshot "—my sisters are *sick* with envy!"

"When are you going on your honeymoon?" Raven asked.

"Tomorrow morning." Charli's expression turned rapturous. "Italy and Greece! I can't wait. I've never been out of the country."

Sunny said, "Amanda told me that Grant named his new boat the *Carlotta*. Is that true?"

Blushing, Charli nodded. Sunny didn't mention what else Amanda had told her—that he'd named the sloop after her "christening," in honor of his wife and the first night they spent together on it.

Grant and Hunter joined them. Hunter came up behind Raven and slid his arms around her waist. She leaned back against him. "Did you tell them our news?" he murmured.

"Not yet." Raven grinned. "We're going to have a baby."

The women squealed in delight. "The first Wedding Ring baby!" Sunny said. "How far along are you?"

"Six weeks." Hunter beamed proudly. "We just found out."

"Congratulations." Grant gave Hunter a hearty handshake and kissed Raven on the cheek. "Charli and I are going to have to work hard to catch up."

"Oh, well, if it's *work*..." Charli teased.

Something behind Sunny snagged Amanda's attention. Amanda tossed a meaningful look to Charli, who elbowed Raven, all of them now pretending not to look. Even the men cast furtive glances over Sunny's shoulder.

"What?" Sunny started to turn toward the entrance to the ballroom.

Amanda grabbed her and spun her back around. "I don't believe I've wished you a happy birthday yet." She gave her a big hug.

"Happy thirtieth birthday, Sunny," Charli said. "What would you like for a birthday present?"

"I'd like to know what's behind me." Amanda and Raven had positioned themselves on either side of Sunny, refusing to let her budge an inch.

"Let me put it this way." Raven squeezed her arm reassuringly. "What do you want more than anything? What have you *always* wanted more than anything?"

A husband.

"Who just came in?" Sunny asked, as her pulse skittered.

Grant turned to Hunter. "They didn't tell her?"

"I believe they're counting on the element of surprise," Hunter said.

"Who?" Sunny demanded, craning her neck without success.

"The Wedding Ring has made its decision," Charli said. "We've chosen a prospective husband for you."

Sunny emitted a squeak of nervous excitement.

"Remember," Raven said. "You're required to give him three months, if he's interested."

"I know the rules," Sunny muttered. "Now, show me my man!"

Her friends swung her around and pointed to a latecomer who hadn't been at the church. He stood in the ballroom's open doorway, scanning the crowd.

A strangled gasp lodged in Sunny's throat. Her heart did the Mexican hat dance as she struggled for air. It was a good thing Raven and Amanda were still holding on to her.

What the hell is he *doing here!*

"Oh no you don't!" Sunny said. "Not him. No way!"

* * *

Don't forget to look out for Sunny's story in **ONE EAGER BRIDE TO GO—** *on the shelves next month.*

Modern Romance™
...seduction and
passion guaranteed

Tender Romance™
...love affairs that
last a lifetime

Sensual Romance™
...sassy, sexy and
seductive

Blaze™
...sultry days and
steamy nights

Medical Romance™
...medical drama on
the pulse

Historical Romance™
...rich, vivid and
passionate

29 new titles every month.

*With all kinds of Romance for
every kind of mood...*

MILLS & BOON®

Makes any time special™

MAT4

0801/123/MB19

OTHER NOVELS BY

PENNY JORDAN

POWER GAMES

POWER PLAY

CRUEL LEGACY

TO LOVE, HONOUR & BETRAY

THE HIDDEN YEARS

THE PERFECT SINNER

MILLS & BOON®